Body in the Barn

A Kate and Doris Mystery

by

Trisha Durrant

For information, email **Cozy Cat Press**, cozycatpress@aol.com or visit our website at: www.cozycatpress.com

COZY CAT
P R E S S

ISBN: 978-1-946063-42-7

Printed in the United States of America
1 2 3 4 5 6 7 8 9 10

For my sister Shirley, the one person with whom I can share everything. Love you, Sis.

Prologue

The overhead lights barely pierced the darkness, the fixtures covered with a thick coating of dust, half the bulbs burned out. It was too much effort for him to pull out the ladder and climb up to replace them.

Out here, away from town, the only outside illumination was the occasional security light at the end of a long driveway. It was an area of scattered ranch houses, built in the fifties, each in the middle of a plot that had once been part of a larger farm. He'd bought the house and land when it was cheap. *Couldn't do that now,* he thought—*all eaten up with new housing additions, one house on top of another.* The wife was always complaining—*why don't we move to Florida and buy a condo—we'd get a good price for this.* But in Florida he'd never be able to get away from her.

He came down to the barn most evenings after supper while the old lady was cleaning up the kitchen. "Going to do some work in the barn," he would say. It was an excuse. The horses were long gone, and the barn empty of all but a few pieces of rusting equipment and broken bales of hay.

She knew why he went down there at night. The magazines were not allowed in the house. No god-fearing man would look at that filth she'd once told him, especially someone who was a deacon in the Baptist church and faithfully attended Sunday service and Wednesday Evening Bible Study every week. He went to a gas station on the edge of town where nobody knew him. There he could get the latest issues, along with a case of beer, something else that was never allowed in the house.

The weak rays of light shone down on the small areas beneath their dusty arcs. Here a rusting wheelbarrow, there a pitchfork leaning over to one side, spot-lit, almost like a stage set. A few feet further on, broken bales of hay, and in between, pools of darkness.

He was sitting in an old armchair that had migrated to the barn after outliving its usefulness as house furniture. His latest magazines were stacked on a hay bale next to his chair along with a six-pack. Leaning back, he popped the top on a cold can of Budweiser, unzipped his jeans and turned the page on his first magazine. A door creaked. He shielded his open crotch with the magazine. "Who's there?" He listened intently but there was only silence.

He turned another page, his breath coming heavier, running his tongue over moist lips. There was a noise, a soft rustling. He stopped, torn between the images on the page and a feeling, an instinct more than anything that someone or something was in the barn with him.

The door crashed back against the wall. The sudden gust raised eddies of dust that danced across the floor. He relaxed. *Just the wind, that's all*. He licked his finger and turned another page.

It was over before his mind had time to process the horror. One minute he was focused on the magazine. The next, he was dimly aware of someone behind him. His head was yanked back against the chair. The can dropped from his hand, spilling beer down the front of his shirt. The gleaming knife slashed into his exposed neck. There was an agonizing burning pain, then nothing. The magazine slid from his lap exposing the open jeans.

The knife flashed once more.

Chapter 1

"Damn it."

There was a crash of books on the other side of the stacks, a set of footsteps retreating hurriedly, and the sound of our staff, break room door slamming shut.

Frank, my fellow volunteer at our beautiful old Carnegie library in the historic heart of Shelbyville, Indiana, turned a shocked face to me. A "damn it" from our library manager, Sebastian, was the equivalent of anyone else dropping the f-bomb.

What in the world was wrong with him now? Usually he was the sunniest personality in the library, always smiling and joking. Other staff members might have a bad day, but never Sebastian. That is, until the last couple of weeks when his personality had undergone a sea change from warm, cuddly teddy bear to snarling tiger. He was ignoring me, one of his best friends at the library, and had snapped at Clarice, our longest-serving volunteer and a real trial to us all. Sebastian, usually unfailingly calm and patient, no matter who he was dealing with, had told her to "get lost" when she went to him with more of her endless complaints. We'd been tiptoeing around him afraid of setting off another explosion. It was time to find out what was wrong.

I whipped around the other side of the shelf, picked up the scattered books and added them to my cart. I could sort and shelve them later.

"I'm taking my break."

That's the great thing about being a volunteer; since you're unpaid, you can take a break whenever you want. They're hardly going to fire you. Sylvia, head librarian and leading lady of our local community theater, looked, nodded, then went back to her computer. She was the very essence of a prim and proper librarian with her sensible shoes, black slacks and bulky sweater, but I happened to know she was checking her Facebook page to which she was addicted. It was either that or e-Harmony. She lived in hopes of finding her soul mate. I'm pretty sure she knew he didn't exist but she loved the hunt.

I put my head around the break room door. Sebastian was sitting at the table, his head in his hands. Tears leaked between his fingers. Frank sat next to him holding a box of tissues and occasionally patting him on the back. He pointed to himself and then Sebastian, to let me know he was taking care of things. I quietly closed the door and left.

Frank was another friend. We had met at the library where he also volunteered. This past year he had been my rock, seeing me through the aftermath of a messy divorce and police investigation, when my sleaze-bag of an ex-husband had been found in my apartment almost at death's door, with the shattered remains of my favorite, antique majolica urn next to him.

Frank had been widowed after a long and happy marriage and was now keeping company—he refused to call it dating—with Margaret, who was wardrobe mistress at the theater.

The break room door opened. Sebastian returned to his desk. His head was down and he refused to make eye contact with anyone. Clearly, he was in no mood to talk.

Frank shrugged his shoulders, gave me a helpless look, and went into the workroom to check in patron holds. I followed him, hoping for a quiet word but there were too many people around, so I finished up my afternoon shift without finding out why Sebastian was having a meltdown.

I live two blocks from the library in the historic part of Shelbyville in a beautiful Queen Anne house. I love the wrap-around front porch, which we fill with wicker furniture and ferns in the summer, the oak double doors with the black and white entry, and the hushed silence that enfolds you as soon as you step inside. It has that aura of peace and serenity that old churches have and I love the feeling of leaving the world behind as soon as the front door closes.

The house had been converted into three apartments. Our artist friends Rose and Enid live on the third floor and use the attic as their studio. I live on the second and my erstwhile roommate, Doris, moved into the first floor when it became available. I found Doris while flying back from a disastrous Hawaiian vacation. She was stranded at the airport so I brought her home with me and somehow she stayed. Since then she had bought the house and become our landlady.

The wind was getting up and the tree outside the stained glass window at the bend of the staircase was moving with it, making red and blue sunbeams dance across the carpet. My apartment door was open, and I could smell the rich aromas of meatloaf and apple pie.

I don't cook very much or very well so I'm lucky Doris is an eighty-year-old human dynamo who does both. I miss her now that she has her own place, but she still probably spends more time in my apartment than her own. Her excuse is that my dog, Digger, is lonely when I'm gone. But since he has the run of the whole house he's hardly ever alone.

"Did you hear what's wrong with Sebastian, Kate?"

I shook my head. Doris is home alone for most of the day and I work practically next to Sebastian, so it's always a mystery to me that she knows about things before I do.

"He and Frank are stopping in for dinner. We'll talk about it then. I asked Rose and Enid, too. I don't suppose Sam will come?" This said wistfully.

Doris loved Sam, my boyfriend, lover, steady date, or whatever the current phrase is. Unfortunately, Sam and I were taking a break at the moment so, as Doris well knew, he was off the dinner guest list.

Sam is a detective with the Shelbyville police department. After a rocky start, our relationship was proceeding smoothly until Sam made the mistake of moving faster than I wanted. I had been divorced for just a year, Sam for over twenty. After a thirty year marriage, I wanted to stretch my wings a little. Sam didn't take the wing stretching too well, hence the taking a break.

The downstairs front door buzzer sounded. I heard Frank and Sebastian's voices over the intercom and let them in. As they came up the stairs, they were joined by Enid and Rose coming down from their third floor apartment. Digger, my rescue dog, trailed along behind them. He saw me and started wagging his tail frantically, dancing around my legs until I knelt to receive my daily quota of sloppy dog kisses.

Sebastian gave me a big hug. "Sorry I've been such a bear lately, it's just…," the tears welled up again. With a sigh, Frank handed him another wad of tissues.

Enid led Sebastian to the armchair in the bay window. Doris handed him a cup of coffee. Rose sat on the arm of the chair and rubbed his back. Digger put his head on his knee and looked up at him with his mournful eyes. Frank stood at the ready with more tissues and I waited for the explanation.

"It's Stephen."

Enough said. Stephen was Sebastian's significant other and also my beautician. He lived and worked in Indianapolis, which was about twenty miles east of Shelbyville, refusing to be, "buried in the country away from all civilization," as he put it. Where Sebastian was soft and caring, Stephen was brittle-edged and volatile. I happened to adore him because underneath the bitchy façade he showed the world was a warm and vulnerable human being.

"He's seeing a new therapist—which is good—you know Stephen has issues. It's dredging up a lot of painful memories and he's not handling it too well. I don't know what to do. He won't meet or talk to me—I think it's over between us."

The tears coursed down his cheeks. Frank did tissue duty again.

Doris rescued the cup before it slipped from Sebastian's fingers and spilled coffee all over the rug. She patted his cheek. "Don't you worry none, my little love. Stephen's going through a bad time now—he needs his space. Give him some time and he'll be fine."

"Do you think that's all it is?"

"I'm sure of it."

And she probably was. I don't know how she did it, but she knew everything. Stephen was a particular favorite of hers. If he confided in anyone it would be Doris.

She made her way to the kitchen, "Let's eat before this meatloaf gets cold."

Chapter 2

The next morning, Doris was knocking at my door before I had drunk my first cup of tea.

"Turn on the television, Kate."

I did as she asked and sat across from her in the den inhaling the milky fragrance of my tea. The local reporter was talking into the camera and gesturing behind her. "A body was discovered early this morning in this barn behind a house out on Route 3. So far the police are refusing to say whether or not foul play was involved."

There was a long shot of a metal pole barn with four police vehicles parked in front. It was too far away to identify any of the people clustered around the gate.

I sipped my tea. I was not at my best first thing in the morning. "What's so important about this that you get me up at the crack of dawn?"

She bristled. "Nothing. I only wondered if you'd heard about it is all." And she left, slamming the door behind her.

What was all that about? Doris knew it took at least two cups of tea before I was fully awake. I groaned. My tea could wait. I'd better apologize for whatever it was I had done. I knocked on her door. She opened it a crack and peered through. Behind her glasses, her eyes were red and watery.

"Can I come in, Doris?"

She said stiffly, "It's not convenient now," and closed the door in my face.

The front doorbell rang. I recognized the two figures silhouetted against the beveled glass. Could this day get any better? I looked down at myself. I was still in my robe and my feet were bare. Oh well, Detective Sam Williamson had seen me in my robe before and out of it too, for that matter. But I hadn't even brushed my hair yet. I briefly flirted with the idea of running upstairs to get dressed but the bell rang once more and with a sigh I opened the door to Sam, my maybe former lover, and Martha, a police officer with our local constabulary, who worked with him.

He stood there with the sun shining on his close cropped silver hair, his button-down shirt reflecting the intense blue of his eyes, razor sharp creases in his khaki slacks and shoes so highly polished I could probably see my face in them. My heart beat a little faster. Sam had that effect on me.

I tried for humor. "Is this official business or did you stop by for breakfast?" The joke fell flat.

Sam's eyes swept over me and then dropped, while Martha gave me a quick smile. "We have a few questions for you. May we come in?"

I led the way upstairs. "Would you like some coffee?"

Martha started to say "yes," but a look from Sam stopped her and, with an apologetic smile at me, she changed her "yes" into "no." Digger came over and rolled on his back, begging for a belly rub. He was the world's most cowardly dog, disappearing whenever strangers came to call, but Sam and Martha were old friends who had rescued him from the streets and found a home for him with me. I saw the look of hurt bewilderment in his soft brown eyes when they ignored him. He left through the dog flap in the kitchen for the back stairs and friendlier folks.

"If you'll excuse me, I'm going to put on some clothes. I wasn't expecting early callers."

Sam stepped forward as if to stop me then turned away.

"Make yourselves at home. I'll only be a couple of minutes.

I quickly hurried down the hallway and put the kettle on for another cup of tea, rushed into the bedroom to throw on some clothes and was dressed and ready before the water boiled. I wandered back into the living room to find Sam and Martha firmly ensconced on the couch so I took the armchair opposite, sipped my tea, and waited for the first question.

"When was the last time you had any contact with Stephen Wills?"

Why was Sam asking about Stephen and why the formality? Stephen was his friend as well as mine.

"Last month when he cut my hair at Jean-Francois; why do you want to know?"

"We're having a hard time contacting him."

Come to think of it, Stephen hadn't been around much lately. A couple of weeks ago we had a meeting at our local community theater to decide on next season's playbill, but Stephen hadn't attended. And he hadn't turned up for dinner, here, the following week, but I wasn't going to tell Sam that. In fact, I wasn't going to tell Sam anything until he told me why he was asking questions about Stephen.

"Why do you want to contact him? Has something happened?"

There was an odd tension in the air. They were both watching my face intently.

Sam ignored the question. "So you haven't seen him in over a month?"

"Sam, I just told you I haven't."

He got to his feet. "If you hear from him, please call us right away. You know the number."

Actually, I had a hair appointment with Stephen the following morning but if Sam wasn't going to volunteer any information, neither would I.

The downstairs door had barely closed behind them both when there was a knock at my door and Doris sidled around it. "Are they gone?"

I nodded. She stood there a moment longer. "Did they say what they wanted?"

"They're looking for Stephen, but won't say why."

"What did you tell Sam?"

"The truth, that I haven't seen Stephen in a month."

"Are they coming back?"

"I don't know, why all the questions?"

"Just asking is all."

And she left, slamming the door behind her once more.

Chapter 3

When I turned up for my monthly cut and color at Jean-Francois' beauty shop in Indianapolis, the whole place was in an uproar.

Jean-Francois, whose real name was Harry Finkel, was snapping at the shampoo girl for not being fast enough. Elsa, who worked the front desk, was dealing with an irate customer while simultaneously talking on the phone. Her face brightened when she saw me—I rarely made a fuss about anything.

She hung up the phone. "We're a little behind, Mrs. Conley. Stephen's not in yet and we can't get hold of him. If you can wait another half hour, Sierra can fit you in. Or if you prefer to wait for Stephen, we can make another appointment for you."

I had no time to ask questions. Elsa was already dealing with the next customer in line. I wandered over to the waiting area. Usually, I was offered coffee or a choice of magazine but nobody seemed to be free. And when I was taken back to the shampoo area it was for a quick wash and rinse without the neck and shoulder massage I had come to expect.

Once I told Sierra the color Stephen used she was quick and competent but completely unable to answer my questions.

"No one knows where he is. He's not called in and there's no answer at his apartment. He's always so reliable. I hope nothing bad has happened."

When I left, they still had not heard from him. I called the library. "Sebastian, I'm worried about

Stephen. The police stopped by my place yesterday morning to ask if I'd seen him, but they wouldn't tell me why. I had an appointment with him today at the shop, but he isn't here and nobody seems able to contact him. I know he lives close by. If you give me his address, I'll go see what I can find out."

Stephen lived further up the block in one of the old apartment buildings that lined Massachusetts Avenue. I was leaning against the window scribbling down the address when I saw a black SUV pass by and park a few spaces up from where I was standing.

I watched a familiar pair of legs, encased in khaki trousers emerge from the driver's side. They were followed by a blue button-down shirt, topped by Sam's distinctive silver hair.

He crossed the street. I followed, staying a few yards behind. I watched him mount the front steps of Stephen's apartment building. He pushed the buzzer, opened the front door and went inside.

I rushed forward to put my foot in the door before it swung completely shut, but I wasn't fast enough. As I was standing on the step trying to find Stephen's name on the list of buzzers, the door opened again and two men came out. I shot past them into the hallway. They made as if to stop me but I quickly said, "Stephen Wills' on the second floor, right?"

Their faces cleared. "Yes, number twenty-one. It's the corner unit, but he's not in."

"Thanks, I'll leave a note on his door."

I looked around and took my bearings. The creaky elevator was slowly winding upward. I waited until I heard it stop and the doors open and close. I crept over to the staircase and started up the stairs. I was cautiously rounding the bend when I saw a pair of feet coming down. They were Sam's.

There really was no place to go. His eyes had that flinty look I knew so well. "What are you doing here?"

What was I, one of his suspects?

"I could ask the same of you."

"I'm here on official business."

The first time I met Sam it was official business involving an attack, by me, on my then husband. In fairness to me, I had caught the said husband humping his new secretary—sorry, personal assistant—in his law office, on top of the antique desk I had bought him for his fiftieth birthday. He had been stupid enough to leave his golf clubs conveniently to hand.

"I stopped by to see Stephen."

"He's not in. Do you know where he is?"

His attitude irked me. "No. I'll come back later."

He caught up with me before I reached the door. "This is not something you should be meddling in, Kate. If you know where he is you need to tell me."

"I don't *need* to do anything, Sam. I told you I don't know. Maybe if you tell me just why it is you want to see him so urgently, I might stop my *meddling* as you call it."

The familiar pulse in his jaw started to throb. "I'm telling you, Kate. Stay out of this." With a muttered, "Excuse me," he pushed past me and exited.

I sighed. Sam was really mad at me. I had a bad feeling that instead of taking a break, we were breaking up.

When I got home, Doris' door was firmly closed and Digger was visiting elsewhere.

Chapter 4

My problems with Sam had started when I told him I was going back to school. Thirty years ago I had given up a college education to put my then husband, Jack, through law school. My mother told me I was stupid to sacrifice my own chance of a future for someone else. In retrospect she was right and I had the divorce to prove it.

At first, Sam thought it a great idea. I applied and was accepted into the Schools of History and Anthropology at IUPUI, the Indianapolis campus of Indiana and Purdue universities. I then signed up for an archaeological dig the school would be conducting over the summer, at a site south of Bloomington. Everything was fine until Sam learned that I would be staying in Bloomington for most of the week and home only on weekends.

We were at Luigi's, our favorite Italian restaurant, when the argument started. We'd had a great dinner and were finishing up the last of a bottle of wine. I was feeling relaxed and mellow until Sam leaned across the table and said casually, "Kate, if you're going to be in Bloomington all summer, we'll hardly see each other. Do you have to do this dig now? There must be lots of other classes you could take that don't involve staying out of town."

For the moment I was speechless. Then I found my voice. "I'm not going to give up the dig in Bloomington just because you might be a little lonely. If you think you're going to miss me that much, take some vacation time and join me there."

His jaw clenched. "I can't do that. I have a job to do."

"And I have a class to take."

From then on it didn't go too well. I might have been a tad antagonistic, but Sam was downright hostile. The upshot was my suggestion that we take a short break from dating. Sam didn't take it too well.

I missed Sam. I liked him—maybe more than liked him—but I was through with sacrificing my wants and needs for someone else's. I had gone from home almost immediately into marriage. This past year was the first time I had ever lived alone. I loved my apartment. I loved my privacy. I loved being in charge of my own life. I didn't want that to change. If Sam couldn't accept it, we were done.

When I arrived for my morning shift at the library, I was immediately waylaid by a determined-looking Sebastian. He grabbed me and almost dragged me into the staff break room.

"Why are the police looking for Stephen? Have you heard from him?"

I rubbed my arm. Sebastian is a lot stronger than he realizes.

"I don't know, and no. I thought you might have some information."

"Your boyfriend came to my house last night and put me through quite an interrogation. He asked a lot of questions but wouldn't say why they were looking for him."

"I went to Stephen's place after my hair appointment yesterday. He wasn't there, but I ran into Sam."

"What did he tell you?"

"Absolutely nothing, except it was not something I should be 'meddling in' and to stay out of it."

Sebastian enclosed me in a big, bear hug. "I'm sorry, Kate. I know things haven't been going too well for you and Sam recently. I'm worried about Stephen. Something's been wrong with him for quite a while, and it's tearing him up inside."

"Nothing seems to be going right lately. Even Doris is mad at me."

"Do you think she knows something about this?"

"I'm afraid to ask in case she bites my head off."

Sebastian went over to the coffee maker on the counter and poured us both a cup. "If anyone knows what's going on it's Doris."

"But she won't tell me anything. She slammed the door in my face when I went to her apartment yesterday morning and I haven't seen her since."

I had barely been home long enough to slip off my shoes and put the kettle on for tea, when there was a tentative knock at my door. It was Doris. She was carrying a blueberry pie—my favorite kind—and she was looking anywhere but at my face.

"Kate, I'm sorry about—you know—how I've been acting."

She still couldn't meet my eyes. "I brought you a pie to go with your tea. Come down and eat dinner with me tonight? I'm making pot roast and mashed potatoes."

I took the pie from her. "Doris, I know something is bothering you. Can't you tell me what it is?"

She shook her head. "No."

"Why not?"

Her eyes filled with tears. "It's best you don't know."

This was not like her. Doris shared everything with me.

"Is it about Stephen? I know Sam is looking for him, but he won't say why."

She stared doggedly at the pie.

"Doris, why can't you tell me?"

"Don't ask me, Kate."

"Is Stephen in some kind of trouble?"

"I already told you. It's best you don't know."

"Why?"

"What you don't know you can't tell."

"Do you mean Sam? We're barely speaking. I won't tell him anything."

"But what if he asks and you have to lie to him? I don't think he could forgive that."

I was beginning to understand. "But what about you? Won't he be just as angry if you lie to him?"

"I don't know where Stephen is now, so I won't be lying."

"But you did know, right?"

She set her mouth and gave a little shake of her head. I knew that look. It meant I'd get nothing more from her.

Chapter 5

Doris' universal panacea was food. She loved to feed people and made all the dishes my grandma used to—chicken and dumplings, ham and beans, chili, macaroni and cheese, pot roast with onion gravy and mashed potatoes—and every kind of pie, cake and bread imaginable. It may not have been the healthiest diet but it sure tasted good and I was looking forward to dinner.

I followed the mouth-watering aroma into the kitchen, calling out her name as I went. Sam was sitting at the table. He rose as I came in.

I looked accusingly at Doris. "You didn't tell me Sam was coming."

She seemed flustered. "Kate, I didn't know. He stopped by a few minutes ago to ask me some questions. He's not staying for dinner."

Sam had a cup of coffee in his hand. "I'll be out of your hair in a minute or two."

I nodded briefly and sat opposite him. Doris placed a cup of coffee in front of me.

"Kate, we're investigating a murder." He sounded apologetic. "I have some questions for Stephen Wills and I'm having a hard time locating him."

"Is it the body in the barn?"

We had few murders in Shelbyville, so it wasn't hard to figure out which one he was talking about.

"Yes. It was a particularly brutal crime…."

Doris blurted out, "I heard someone cut his thingie off."

Sam had just taken a big swig of his coffee. He took a deep breath, choked, and sprayed coffee all over the table. He coughed and spluttered, fighting to catch his breath. When he was finally able to speak, he zeroed in on Doris.

"Where did you hear that? We never released that detail."

"I don't know."

"Who told you?"

By this time he was standing over her.

"I must have heard it somewhere."

His tone turned icy, "Where?"

Doris dabbed at her eyes with a napkin. "Don't yell at me, Sam."

She covered her face with her hands and her shoulders started to shake.

I couldn't let this go on. "Stop it, you big bully. She told you she doesn't know. Just leave."

He turned his glare on me. I glared back. He took a deep breath and stalked out, slamming the door behind him.

Doris perked up right away. "Oh good. Thanks for getting rid of him."

"Doris, you're not upset?"

She grinned at me. "I didn't lie to him, did I?"

The next day I was grabbing a quick lunch at the deli on the square when I heard the jangle of the bell on the door. I looked up to see Sam and Martha framed in the doorway. Sam stopped abruptly when he saw me and Martha almost ran into the back of him. She gave me a brief wave and started threading her way through the tables toward me. Sam reluctantly followed.

Before they got to me, I heard, "Kate, darling. How are you? I haven't seen you in an age."

There, looming over my table, on the ridiculously high heels she wore in a vain attempt to make her squat body look taller and more slender, was one of my least favorite people, Bitch Barbara, the wife of my ex-husband's accountant. Barbara was as sweet as honey and as deadly as a viper. It was she who'd announced my then husband's affair, with his new and very young personal assistant, in front of everyone at a museum board luncheon, at the country club. And she'd had the gall to pat my hand and commiserate with me while her beady little eyes gleamed with satisfaction at the shocked reaction she had generated.

The Bitch had a particularly penetrating voice. "Are you and Dusty getting back together?"

I was astounded. "Dusty?"

Where did that come from? Dusty was someone I had dated in high school. I hadn't seen or thought about him in almost thirty years.

"Well, you know he's running the dig you've signed up for. I had a long conversation with his sister. She thinks, since you're both divorced, you'll get back together. After all, Dusty will be here all summer."

She noticed Sam standing beside her with a shell-shocked look on his face.

She smiled sweetly at him. "Kate and Dusty dated all through high school. He was the love of her life and everyone thought they would end up marrying."

She turned her fake smile on me. "I know how devastated you were when he dumped you for someone else. You married Jack on the rebound, didn't you?"

The look of betrayal on Sam's face told her all she needed to know. She put her hand up to her mouth to stifle a giggle. "Oops, I'm so sorry. I seem to have spoken out of turn. I'd better leave. Goodbye, darling, and good luck with Dusty." She tottered off, happy that her venom had found such an easy target.

Sam sank into the chair opposite me. His voice was low and harsh. "When were you going to tell me that you were hooking up with an old boyfriend—what did she say—the love of your life?"

His anger was palpable, his body almost vibrating with it.

"Sam, there's nothing to tell. The syllabus had the instructor listed as Wendell Carter. I never connected that name with the Dusty I used to know."

I could tell he didn't believe me. He got up so abruptly his chair almost fell over. The next thing I heard was the slam of the diner door. And Sam walked out of my life.

Chapter 6

Dusty and I had dated all through high school. We were inseparable. Archaeology was his passion and became mine. We spent hours tramping over his father's fields after the spring plowing, looking for arrowheads and any other artifacts that had been churned up by the rotating blades. We took our finds to the library, devouring every book we could find on the Native American tribes who had peopled the fertile land on which we now lived. Our ambition was to become famous archaeologists and travel the world together digging up ancient sites.

Dusty graduated the year before I did and attended Indiana University, Bloomington. This was before cell phones and Facebook, but we kept in touch by writing almost daily.

At first he wrote how much he missed me, how he looked forward to summer so we could be together again. Then the name Helen began to creep into his letters. He and Helen were working in the lab together. Helen was brilliant and he was learning so much from her.

I became madly jealous of this mysterious Helen. Hoping to generate that same jealousy in Dusty, I wrote to him and suggested we should see other people for a while. The captain of the wrestling team had asked me out. I told Dusty I was going to accept.

I thought he would write back immediately, swear undying love, and beg me not to date anyone else. I was wrong. I never heard from him again. He transferred to a school in Arizona, and later I heard he had married a fellow student. Helen turned out to be Dusty's anthropology professor and was old, at least sixty. Dating the wrestling team captain lasted until his first meet when I saw him sweating and grunting in his disgusting uniform.

I graduated, attended IU until I met Jack, married him, and dropped out of school.

It's unsettling when a piece of your past that was over and done with intrudes on your present-day life. I was sitting at my kitchen table, poring over the syllabus from IUPUI, trying to figure out how I could have missed Dusty's name. Then I saw it. The professor for the course I would be taking was listed as D. Wendell Carter, Ph.D. I suppose I had once known that Wendell was Dusty's middle name, but it was a name he hated and never used. So I hadn't made the connection.

Now that I did know, what was I going to do? And how could I explain it to Sam? Did I even want to? Our relationship seemed to be over even before Bitch Barbara had dripped her honeyed venom in his ear. I had told Sam the truth. That I didn't know a former boyfriend was teaching the summer course. If he chose to believe I was lying, that was his problem, not mine.

But should I still take the class? What if Dusty thought the only reason I signed up for the dig was to meet him again? I would have to think about this.

There was a knock at my door. Doris popped into the living room. "Kate, you're still going to audition for Sebastian's play, aren't you?"

I had completely forgotten that auditions for our local community theater were set for this week.

"I meant to read the play first to see if there's any part suitable for me."

"Sebastian wants you to be there, so he must have something in mind."

I'd made my stage debut a few months earlier, playing a slutty maid, which had been a big success and resulted in my being bitten by the acting bug. I made a mental note to check out a copy of the play from the library.

Doris stood at the end of the kitchen counter, tidying up a pile of mail that had yet to find its way to my desk in the den. She obviously had something she wanted to say to me. I waited her out. She would get to it in her own time.

"Kate, I don't want to interfere..."

Which meant she was going to.

"I heard about that woman—you know—the nasty one you call the Bitch, and what she said to you in the diner in front of Sam." She hesitated then went on. "What are you going to do?"

"About what, Doris?"

"That dig thing. Are you still going to do it?"

"Do you think I should?"

"It's just...Sam's a good man. You'll never find a better. What if this breaks you up?"

"We're already broken up."

"No, I mean permanently."

Doris loved Sam. He had helped her a few months ago when she was in a bad situation with her estranged son. She looked at me with eyes that reminded me of Digger begging for a treat.

Before I could answer, the phone rang. The voice was deeper and huskier now, but I recognized it immediately.

"Hi, Kate, it's been a long time."

Chapter 7

"Dusty?"

Doris remained rooted to the spot. I held the phone against my shoulder. "Doris, could I have a little privacy?"

She gave one of her sniffs and left. At least she didn't slam the door this time.

The disembodied voice said, "Are you still there?"

I quickly put the phone to my ear. "Yes. I'm surprised to hear from you after all these years."

"But you signed up for my dig." He sounded slightly exasperated.

"I had no idea then that the Dusty I used to know was Professor Wendell Carter. I only recently made the connection. When did you start using your middle name?"

"When I realized that an archaeologist named Dusty probably wouldn't be taken as seriously as one named Wendell."

There was a long pause. "Kate, I've always regretted the way things ended between us. I was young and immature. Later, I sent you an apology but you never answered."

The day the letter arrived had been gray and dreary with lowering skies and a chance of snow. My daughter, Ellie, was a few months old, teething and fretful. I was having a hard time adjusting to being a stay-at-home mother.

The envelope had been postmarked Belize. It was crumpled and festooned with colorful stamps. Dusty wrote that he was sitting next to a campfire drinking beer and thinking of me. He was working on a Mayan site discovered the previous year. He described the surrounding jungle, the colorful flowers that perfumed the air, the sound of screaming monkeys and the brilliant flashes of color as birds darted from tree to tree. As I read, I could see the lush foliage, almost taste the rich, jungle smells. For a brief moment I saw myself with Ellie in a sling on my back, tramping the path toward a magnificent, vine-covered ruin, Dusty at my side, his arm around my shoulders, mine around his waist. The way we used to be.

I looked outside at the gloomy weather, envisioned the warmth and bright sun of a tropical paradise and for a brief moment I was tempted. Then I threw the letter in the fire and put away all thoughts of Dusty and an exotic life-style.

He waited. I said nothing.

Finally, he asked, "Kate, why don't we have dinner and catch up on everything?"

"Well…"

My first reaction was to refuse. Then I thought, why not talk with Dusty before deciding whether or not to spend the summer in Bloomington?

"Where shall we meet?"

We fixed a place and time for the following evening.

At least it wasn't Luigi's, but I was surprised that Dusty wanted to meet in Indianapolis rather than Shelbyville. When I got to the restaurant he was sitting at a table in the back.

He waved me over. "Kate, you haven't changed a bit from high school."

I laughed. "Nice of you to say so, but hardly true."

I couldn't say the same about him. It wasn't that his hair was thinning and his face was somewhat lined, it was something internal. Dusty had always had a big grin, an enjoyment of life that was infectious. But no more— it was as if a light had switched off inside him.

The waiter came to take our order, and his chirpy attitude got us through the first few awkward minutes. Wine might have eased the strain, but I had driven so I didn't order anything to drink. Dusty didn't either.

I decided to plunge right in. "Dusty, did you know that your sister is going around telling people that since we are both divorced we're going to get back together? It's a little embarrassing. The only reason I'm taking your class is because I quit college to put my former husband through law school. Now I want to make up for lost time. Archeology was my passion in high school so I thought I'd start with that."

His eyes narrowed. "My sister would never say something like that. When did you see her?"

I didn't understand why his tone had turned so hostile. "I didn't see her. A friend of hers, Barbara Armstrong, announced it in front of the whole deli where I was having lunch the other day. She said she heard it from your sister. The guy I was dating didn't take it too well."

"Barbara Armstrong is hardly a friend. My sister loathes her. There's no way she would even talk to her, let alone discuss something so personal."

"Yes, Barbara's somewhat of a bi... gossip. Anyway, I'm glad it isn't true. I'm excited to be finally participating in an actual dig."

"Kate, our relationship can be only that of teacher and student. And I'd prefer if you wouldn't tell anyone that we once dated."

Did Dusty think I was expecting to pick up where we had left off, all those years ago? I took a deep breath. "Dusty, you asked me to meet you, not the other way around. I can certainly keep our relationship on a strictly professional level."

"When you signed up for the dig, you honestly didn't know I was running it?"

His line of questioning annoyed me. "I've already told you, I honestly didn't know."

"Have you followed my academic career at all?"

"No, but I'm glad you followed the career path you wanted."

His fingers restlessly drummed the table. "So you know nothing of where I've lived or worked in the past thirty years?"

He watched me intently.

"Dusty, before I graduated high school, you transferred to a school in Arizona and married a fellow student. I received a letter from you a few years later. You wrote that you were working on a dig in Belize. By then, I was married with a new baby and never got around to answering it."

He was silent for a few moments, then, "Kate, if I tell you something in confidence, will you promise to not tell another soul?"

He looked intently into my eyes. He was deathly serious.

"I promise."

"I'm not divorced."

I sat back in my chair. "Why would you tell everyone that you are? Why the deception?"

"I'm being stalked."

"Stalked?" I could hardly believe what I was hearing.

"My first marriage lasted less than a year. I was single until I met Sheila. We were married six years ago. When we got back from our honeymoon there were three letters waiting for me at school. They were rambling nonsense, something about her not being the right wife for me. I threw them in the trash. Earlier this year, we had our first child, a girl, and that's when this nightmare started."

The waiter brought our entrees. Dusty pushed his to one side and leaned his elbows on the table. "At first, I didn't take it seriously. Over the years you get the needy students, the ones who have a crush on their professor and are in the office almost every day wanting attention. That's what I thought this was. You learn how to deal with it and defuse the situation, but this was different."

He took a sip of his water. "A letter came to my office right after Lily was born. It was more rambling nonsense but the gist of it was that I had made a big mistake."

His hands started to shake and he put his glass down with a crash. "Three days later there was another. This one mentioned Lily by name. It said I was lucky she was still healthy. No more than that, but I was concerned. Then our dog disappeared. Two days later, Sheila found his body in the backyard. His throat had been cut and he'd been hacked to pieces. That's when we realized that whoever was sending the letters was dangerous and also knew where we lived. My wife and I talked it over. We decided that until the police caught whoever was doing this, for Lily's safety we would split up. I decided to come back to Indiana and tell everyone I was divorced. Sheila took Lily and went to stay with her parents in North Carolina."

"Dusty, I'm so sorry. Do the police have any idea who it is?"

"I've given them the names of all my students from the past six years and anyone else I could think of, including my ex-wife."

"Was that why you asked if I had followed your career?"

His face turned red. "The police asked for the names of everyone I had ever dated. We'd had no contact since high school but still…"

"But still? Did you really suspect me?"

"My sister told me you'd once been arrested for attacking your husband."

"I caught him having sex with his personal assistant on top of the antique desk I bought him for his fiftieth birthday. His golf clubs were right next to the door. Any woman would have done what I did."

"I'm sorry, Kate; the police have very little to go on. I destroyed the first letters because I thought it would go away on its own. After the dog incident," his eyes filled with tears and he blinked them away, "I had to get them involved. I gave them your name because we once dated. Also you had signed up for the dig. This person is totally unbalanced. If you decide to work in Bloomington, for your own safety, it would be better if we acted like complete strangers. And you'll have to call me Wendell."

Chapter 8

I drove home with my mind churning. How sad that Dusty had to be separated from his wife and baby because a crazy person had some kind of obsession with him. He had emphasized that I should do some serious thinking before deciding whether or not to spend the summer in Bloomington working on his dig. I intended to. I had no desire to be the target of some maniacal stalker.

But this would be the first season of the excavation. I hated to miss it. On the other hand, if a dangerous lunatic was lurking around the site and learned that Dusty and I had once dated, would that put me in danger? I was so immersed in my thoughts I must have been on auto-pilot. I pulled myself together and took in my surroundings. I was almost home. Luigi's was just ahead on the left. Two people were going up the shallow, front steps. The woman stumbled and the man put a protective hand under her elbow. She smiled up at him as he opened the door. The light spilled out from the restaurant highlighting his silver hair. It was Sam.

I stopped the car and leaned over the steering wheel trying to catch my breath. I had known since the day in the deli that my relationship with Sam was probably over. What I didn't expect was that he would move on so quickly and with a friend of mine, Pamela Moore.

Before Sam and I had started dating, I had briefly gone out with Pamela's abusive ex-husband but dropped him immediately when I found out what kind of man he was. Doris and I had felt sorry for Pamela, as we would for any woman trapped in a bad relationship, and we tried to include her in our circle of friends. Evidently, we had succeeded beyond my wildest dreams.

The house was dark when I finally arrived home. I needed Doris to make a cup of tea for me and tell me everything was going to be all right but she was already in bed. I sat on the couch feeling utterly alone. Digger came over and put his head on my knee. He looked up at me with his mournful eyes. I rubbed his ears, and he licked my hand.

At least Digger still loved me.

I tried to be excited about auditioning for the new play. It was set to open the week before I left for Bloomington. After that, I would have to get back into town on Friday afternoons and leave again after the Sunday matinees. It would be hectic but do-able.

I was alone again. Doris had gone to the theater early to discuss costumes with Margaret. Enid was designing the set and meeting with her stage crew, so they rode together and I told them I would follow later.

The parking lot was full when I got there. There was an open spot on the street in front of the theater so I took it and entered through the side door. A cacophony of sound greeted my ears, shrieking laughter, animated conversations and people yelling across the auditorium as they saw someone they knew.

I stayed in the doorway and searched the crowd for familiar faces. The first person I saw was Sam with Pamela Moore by his side. They were engaged in an intense conversation. She gave him a tremulous smile and he smiled back. I felt betrayed and angry, which was stupid. My relationship with Sam was over. He could date anyone he wanted.

I couldn't face seeing them together. I turned, walked out, got in my car and drove back home.

The next morning, Doris knocked at my door, bearing bagels for breakfast. "What happened to you last night? I thought you were going to audition. Sebastian was disappointed that you weren't there."

I busied myself putting the kettle on for tea. Doris would see by my face that something was wrong. When I had myself under control, I turned and answered her. "I decided it was going to be too difficult to work around my school schedule. I'll explain things to Sebastian when I see him at the library this afternoon."

"You should have come anyway. Everyone was asking about you."

"I'm sorry, Doris. It was a last minute decision."

I poured boiling water into the teapot and sat down at the table opposite her.

"Kate, you'll never guess who got the part Sebastian wanted you to play."

"Who was it?"

"Pamela Moore; can you believe it?"

So she got my part, too. I decided to spend the summer in Bloomington.

Chapter 9

I was on my knees with my head in the back of the hall closet, dragging out a suitcase to take to IU, when I heard a pounding on my door. At the same time the downstairs buzzer sounded. I dropped the suitcase in the middle of the hallway, pressed the button on the intercom and opened the door with my other hand.

Doris rushed in, almost knocking me over. "Kate, they've found Stephen's car." She sounded panic stricken.

A familiar voice over the intercom said, "Detective Williamson. We're downstairs. Would you please let us in?"

I pressed the buzzer to open the front door and quickly asked, "Where was it found?"

Before she could answer, I heard the heavy tread of feet on the stairs. Sam and Martha, along with Kevin, a young detective with the department who was engaged to Sam's daughter, Mira, stepped into my apartment. In better days, Doris and I had been invited to the wedding, but the way things were between Sam and me, I didn't know if the invitation still held.

Kevin almost tripped over the bag I had dragged out. He laughed. "Going somewhere, Kate?"

Sam glared at him and turned to me. "I hope you don't mind. We have a few questions for you."

I led him into the living room with a chastened Kevin trailing us.

Sam waited until Doris and I sat on the couch then stood in front of us as if we were naughty children about to get a lecture from the principal.

He cleared his throat. "We found Stephen Will's car at the theater."

He waited for a reaction. Getting none, he went on, "Do either of you know how it got there?"

My conscience was clear. "No, I have no idea."

He looked at Doris.

"No, I don't know nothin' about it neither. Where was it?"

"In the storage garage behind the theater, where the flats are kept. Someone had arranged the scenery around it so it couldn't be seen from the window."

I shrugged my shoulders. "I've never been in that building."

Doris echoed me. "Nor me."

"So neither of you know how the car got there or where Stephen Wills is staying right now?"

Doris and I both shook our heads.

His laser eyes scanned our faces. "Then you wouldn't mind if we checked your apartments?"

Doris sniffed. "You got one of them search warrants?"

"Do we need one?"

"No, I got nothin' to hide. Just don't make a mess."

Sam looked at me.

"Go ahead if it means you'll stop bothering us."

He nodded to Kevin and Martha. I heard Kevin go up the stairs to Rose and Enid's apartment while Martha followed Doris.

I sat on the couch and picked up a magazine.

Sam stood there uncertainly for a moment. "You don't want to come with me?"

"No, but as Doris said, don't make a mess."

He went through the pocket doors and disappeared into the dining room. I heard him go into the kitchen. The back door opened and his footsteps echoed down the stairs. A few minutes later, I heard him walking through the hallway and he came back into the living room.

I looked up from the magazine I was pretending to read. "Are you satisfied I'm not harboring a fugitive?"

"Kate," his voice had a pleading note, "I have a murder to solve and Stephen Wills was at the victim's house close to the time the murder took place."

He watched my face. I said nothing, so he went on, "And someone connected to the theater must have known about the car in the garage."

"Not necessarily. Stephen has keys to all the buildings. He could have hidden the car in the storage garage himself. How did you find it? "

"I was at the theater this morning when the stage crew hauled out the flats for their next production. One of the guys moved a piece of scenery and there it was."

"So are you through harassing us?"

Sam sat in the chair opposite the couch. He leaned forward. I kept reading. I heard him sigh. "How did we get to this point, Kate? Can't we talk about it?"

I flipped over a page. "There's nothing to discuss."

"I know that I shouldn't have asked you to give up the dig. We were…"

He paused. Sam was uncomfortable talking about personal issues.

"Things were going well for us and I didn't want that to stop. When you said you were going to be away for most of the summer, I sort of panicked. I'm sorry we got into that big argument. I didn't realize it was so important to you. If I could take back what I said, I would."

If he had stopped right then who knows what would have happened but he kept talking. "If you'd told me your former boyfriend was going to be in Bloomington with you, I wouldn't have been so angry that day in the diner. It was the fact that you kept it from me."

I gritted my teeth and forced out the words. "I told you I didn't know Dusty was in charge of the dig. If you choose to believe I'm lying there's nothing more to say."

I walked over to the door and held it open. "Goodbye, Sam."

He started to argue, saw my face, and left.

I didn't waste any sympathy on him because a couple of hours later, when I was driving to the library for my afternoon shift, I saw him coming out of the deli on the square with Pamela Moore. Sam had made a fast recovery.

Chapter 10

That evening I went downstairs to talk to Doris. She was sitting on her couch, staring into space, with Digger lying next to her.

"Doris, can I ask you something?"

She jumped, startled. She had been lost in thought and hadn't heard me enter.

"Sam told me Stephen went to the murdered man's house the night he was killed."

She nodded. "I know about that."

"When you came up to my apartment to listen to the TV news about the murder, Stephen was at your place. That's why you wouldn't let me in when I came down here to see why I had upset you, right?"

She took a deep breath. "He came to me the night it happened. He was so scared he didn't know where to go. Kate, he didn't kill that man. He was already dead when Stephen found him. He said it was an awful thing to see."

Her eyes filled with tears that spilled over and ran down her wrinkled cheeks. Digger gave a soft whine and licked the side of her face. She stroked his ears and he settled down again. "The man was his uncle. He was a—you know—one of those people who abuse children."

She added, "Not just hitting them."

It took a moment to get what she was saying.

"You mean a child molester?"

"Yes. One of them. Stephen used to stay with him and his aunt during summer, school vacation. His parents thought it was good for him because the uncle had a bunch of horses and was going to teach him to ride. He wouldn't say anything about what happened. He just told me he was going to therapy and one of the things his therapist told him was to confront his abuser. She said it would give him—oh, what's the word—auto something."

"Autonomy?"

"Yes, that's it. It would help him get over it—have power over it or something. Anyway, that's why he went there that night. He saw the light in the barn and drove down there. He didn't want to go in but he finally did and found the uncle sitting in a chair with his throat slashed and—the other thing."

"You mean the…?" I couldn't quite bring myself to say the word.

Doris nodded. "Yeah, that. There was blood everywhere. Stephen said he almost passed out but when he pulled himself together, I was the first person he thought of so he came here. I told him Sam would help him but he was hysterical. I put him to bed in the spare room. I thought we all could talk to him when he calmed down a bit."

"So when Sam and Martha came to the house that morning he was in your apartment?"

"Yes."

"Why didn't you tell me? I could have helped you."

"You and Sam were dating…" I tried to interrupt but she went on. "It wouldn't have been fair to ask you to hide it from him so it was best I kept it from you."

"When did you hide the car at the theater?"

"I didn't. Stephen must have done that. After Sam came to your apartment that day, he told me he'd find another place to stay and begged me not to tell anyone he'd been here. I went to my quilting circle that afternoon and when I came back he was gone. He must be hid real good because the police have been checking everywhere. I want to help him but I don't know the best thing to do."

I hugged her. "It will all work itself out. Just wait and see."

I was packing for the dig. Long-sleeved shirts, jeans, sun hat, bandanas, sun block, rubbing alcohol, baby oil, a trowel, boots and sturdy sneakers, bedding, towels— the list seemed endless. We would be staying in dorm rooms on the IU campus. I briefly wondered if I would have to share a room.

There was a quiet knock at my door. Doris walked in. She looked at my partially-filled suitcase, gave one of her sniffs and said, "I just came up to tell you I decided not to buy a gun."

I sat back on my heels in surprise. Doris had been talking about getting a gun since my apartment had been broken into the previous summer. Enid, Rose and I, had been trying to talk her out of it ever since. She hadn't mentioned it in a while and I thought she had forgotten about it.

"I was never keen on the idea, Doris. I think guns are dangerous."

She sighed. "We had a situation at the gun range today."

That grabbed my attention. "You told me you gave up your shooting classes."

"With you going so far away, I thought maybe I should try again."

She made it sound as if I were going to Siberia instead of southern Indiana.

"What happened?"

"There was a really big man next to me and he was taking up most of my space." She sounded defensive. "Anyway, he was too close to me and when I stepped back to aim he backed into me just as I was about to pull the trigger. He jogged my arm and made me drop the gun." She took a deep breath. "It went off. The bullet didn't hit him anywhere but he screamed and fell over backwards and hit his head." She added, "It was his fault. He should have kept out of my way but he blamed me."

She settled herself on the sofa in the living room. "There's too many safety things with guns. I'm thinking of something easier. My instructor said I could buy it online without all that dang paperwork."

For a moment I panicked, thinking of all the lethal weapons that could be bought over the internet, but when she said it was small enough to carry in her purse, I calmed down.

"Can I ask what it is?"

She set her mouth. "Not yet. I gotta think about it first."

She wandered back into the hallway and looked down at my suitcase. "So you're still going?"

"Doris, it's only for six weeks and I'll be home every weekend. The time will fly by."

"Have you talked to Sam about it? Martha says he's real upset about you breaking up with him."

I'd have believed that if he hadn't hooked up with Pamela Moore right after our last contentious encounter when he'd accused me of lying. He'd had his chance and blown it.

I didn't want to share the details with Doris. Instead I said, "Sam's moved on. He's dating someone else. I've seen them together a couple of times."

"Who is it?"

"Let's not talk about it now. Why don't you help me check this list to make sure I'm not forgetting anything?"

And we settled down to packing my suitcase.

Chapter 11

My arms were aching from hauling an overstuffed bag of bedding and a heavy suitcase up two flights of stairs. I was trying to get everything from the car in one trip.

"Hi, do you need some help?"

I turned a little too quickly. The voice belonged to a blond, handsome, tanned individual, armed with a clipboard and a devastating smile.

For a moment, I felt slightly dizzy. I tried not to pant but I'd just climbed two flights of stairs. "I'm looking for my room."

"She's one of mine, Adrian."

I turned. The stockily-built woman was shorter than me. She was dressed in baggy jeans and a faded t-shirt. A ball cap covered her short, cropped hair. Her face had the texture of tanned leather. Her smile was friendly but far from devastating.

"You must be Kate Conley, right?"

I acknowledged that I was and she took my suitcase from me.

"I'm Sal. Follow me. I've put you down here at the end."

The gorgeous Adrian gave me a dazzling smile. "See you later." And he turned toward an elevator, which I had somehow missed, to greet the next new arrivals.

I hurried after my suitcase.

"I'm one of the team leaders. There are three of us and Dr. Carter. He's in charge."

She moved at a rapid clip down the corridor and I was too out of breath to answer her. It didn't matter anyway, she just kept talking. "Here's your room. It's quieter here—no foot traffic past your door. I'm right here opposite you." She waved at the door across the hall. "The kids can get a little noisy sometimes but during the week they're usually exhausted after digging all day so they crash early."

She opened the last door in the hallway and disappeared inside. I followed.

She handed me a sheet of paper. "Here's a daily schedule for you. There's one dining hall open for us, directions are at the bottom of the page and we're meeting there at six. You can go off campus to eat if you want, but by the time you get back from the field, take a shower and check for ticks, most people just want to eat and sleep."

"Ticks?"

"Yeah, you brought baby oil and cotton balls in your kit, right?"

There was a noise outside. "Gotta go. We'll talk about everything in orientation tonight. See you then."

I looked around the room. The floor was covered with the same dingy brown tile as the corridor outside. There were plastic blinds over the one window. The bed and mattress were against the wall. Only one bed, I noted. The closet was open. No hangers. I made a mental note to bring some next time. A three-drawer dresser, and a chipped desk with chair, completed the furnishings. Not much had changed since I was last at IU.

I started unrolling the bedding. This was going to be fun—except for the ticks.

Later that evening at dinner, I found that college food had improved immensely since my undergrad days. Instead of the stodgy, mostly canned meals I remembered, there was a variety of food with lots of fresh vegetables and salads. Since I was the only non-traditional freshman, Sal invited me to sit at her table with Adrian and Cynthia, the other team leaders.

I stuck out my hand. "Hi, I'm Kate Conley."

Cynthia ignored me and turned to say something to Adrian. He immediately jumped up, pulled out the chair between himself and Cynthia, and held it for me to sit. I thanked him and was rewarded with another dazzling smile, which elicited a sullen frown from her.

"Are you all settled in? Any questions?"

I smiled back. He really was a gorgeous man. "Only one, but it's for Sal."

I turned to her. "Earlier you said something about ticks and baby oil."

She laughed. "Didn't mean to scare you. You have to watch for ticks. They're in the brush and trees at the edge of the field. That's another reason you need a hat. They're a bugger to get out if they get into your scalp. Just check yourself when you shower at the end of the day. If you find one, don't try to pull it off with tweezers. Put some baby oil on a cotton ball, hold it over the tick and it will back right out. They breathe through their skin so it's an easy way to get rid of them."

There was the sound of a fork tinkling against a glass. Immediately the students quieted down and Dusty stood to start the orientation.

Chapter 12

I collapsed on my bed. The first day had been brutal.
There was no shade and the temperature was in the 90's
with humidity as high. The site was laid out in a grid
and we students were assigned blocks. Our task was to
check every square inch of ground and bag and label
whatever we found. My haul, after a morning's work of
bending over and scanning the sandy dirt, was one
empty bag that had held chips—barbeque flavor—four
pebbles of varying sizes, an assortment of twigs and a
piece, almost a flake, of pottery too small to identify
with the naked eye.

The sullen Cynthia was supervising us and Sal had
to come by and remind her to give us water breaks,
which she grudgingly did.

Sal had turned to me. "Kate, the back of your neck is
getting sunburned. Wet your bandana and cover it
otherwise you're going to be pretty sore tonight."

As she walked away she said, "Keep water on it,
you'll feel better."

She was right. Cynthia scowled every time I went
back to the water cooler but it was my neck. I looked
for the gorgeous Adrian. He was working at the far
corner of the field with Dusty. They had a piece of
equipment that they were running over the surface of
the ground. It looked like a box on wheels and Dusty
had some contraption hanging from his neck that he and
Adrian consulted every few yards.

I turned to the tiny, blonde student working next to
me. "What are they doing over there?"

"GPR." When she saw the bewildered look on my face she took pity on me and explained. "Ground penetrating radar. They run it over the surface and it picks up any anomalies. From the read-out they decide where we are going to dig."

"Anomalies?"

"Pipes, stone foundations, bones, pottery—sort of like an x-ray of the ground. Next they'll mark out specific areas to dig. That's when the real fun starts."

She laughed. "Technology is great but on my first dig my team leader handed me a bent coat hanger and told me to hold it out in front of me and walk over a certain spot. I did and at one point I felt something— almost like a magnetic force—pull the hanger down toward the ground. When we actually started digging we found pottery remains."

"Is that like water dowsing? You think that's for real?"

"All I know is that it was an ordinary metal coat hanger and I definitely felt it move in my hands. I'm Dawna by the way. We're both on Sal's team."

"I'm Kate. You've been on digs before?"

"This is my third season working with Wendell. The first two seasons were in Belize. He's been working on this one site there for years. I don't know why he wanted to switch to Indiana this season, 12th century Late Woodland Indians aren't nearly as interesting as the Mayans."

"Why did you come then?"

"I like working with him. The professor who took over in Belize is a total jerk." She stopped. "Don't tell anyone I said that; I may have to work for him again at some point."

I laughed. "I'm a novice and I don't know anybody. I'm glad I'm on Sal's team though."

I looked up. Cynthia was scowling at me again. Luckily, we broke for lunch right then. Dusty and Adrian did some complicated things with surveying instruments while I started to fill out the journal I had to keep of my daily activities. The rest of the day was taken up with completing the ground survey.

We got back to the dorms, filthy and exhausted. I headed to the showers where I checked every inch of my body for ticks. Thankfully I was tick-free.

As I lay on the bed, there was a pounding on my door. "Kate, are you planning on eating with us?"

It was Sal. I was planning on sleeping the night away but food suddenly sounded really good.

"I'll be right there."

Chapter 13

The days fell into a rhythm. I'd wake up, briefly toy with the idea of skipping breakfast in order to grab another half hour of sleep then get up anyway because I needed tea.

In addition to Dawna, there were two more students on my team: Greg, who was an earnest young man of about twenty and Leslie, a tall, dark-haired, grad student who had also been with Dusty in Belize. We worked in pairs. One of us would dig while the other hauled out the dirt for screening. By the end of the day, my knees were sore from kneeling on the rough ground. My back and arms ached from hauling heavy buckets of dirt out of the excavation and lifting them up onto the screen.

I was gently scraping my trowel over the bottom of the hole we had dug when I heard a little chink. My trowel had struck something. I gently loosened the soil around whatever it was and smoothed it away with my hands. It was a shard of pottery.

"I've found something."

Leslie and Greg crowded around me.

Dawna was screening the bucket of earth I had dug out of our pit. She pulled something small from the top of the screen and held it up. "I've found something too."

Dusty and Sal hurried over. Sal poured water over Dawna's find to wash off the dirt and examine it more closely, while Dusty jumped into the hole and looked at the shards of pottery I'd unearthed.

He knelt next to me and brushed the soil off one of the pieces. "Good work, Kate. It's a piece of gouache pottery—look at the design on it. Take your time. When you've uncovered the rest of it give me a call."

He left and I forgot about my aching back and knees. The adrenaline coursed through my body. I found more pieces and carefully documented their placement in my field notebook. Leslie had a bagful of tiny shards that she had picked out of the screen.

Greg pushed up his glasses which kept sliding down his sweaty nose. "Kate, it looks as if you might have a pot there, maybe enough to reconstruct."

A whole pot! I resisted the temptation to tear into the pit. We methodically kept working. Leslie was the one who found the stained earth. "Look at this. It looks like a post-hole stain. Maybe we've found a dwelling."

A dwelling and pottery, none of us wanted to stop. But our driver was impatiently honking his horn so we documented everything, reluctantly dragged a tarp over the site and got into the van for our trip back to the dorm.

The first week flew by. We dug up the rest of the pottery shards and Greg was excitedly babbling on about piecing them together. Pottery was his passion. We found more organic stains but because of the pattern they formed, Sal thought they could be part of a village palisade, rather than a dwelling.

"It's the perfect location for a palisaded village. There's White River over there." She waved at the river in the distance. "And just behind the hedgerow over here is a stream. The river would be for transportation and the stream would be close by for water."

We'd already learned that the flint used in making arrowheads, found by one of the other teams, had come from neighboring Ohio, possibly by canoe down White River.

Dawna, Greg, Leslie and I had turned into a close-knit team. I was torn. I wanted to get back to Shelbyville for the weekend to see Digger and all my friends but I didn't want to miss anything.

Sal decided for me. "Go home, Kate. We're all taking the weekend off. You're not going to miss a thing."

When I got back to Shelbyville the house was empty. Even Digger was gone. My apartment had a forlorn feel to it, as if it felt as neglected as I did. I didn't expect to be greeted by a group of flag-waving friends but I thought someone might have been there.

The weekend before I drove down to Bloomington had been the opening of Sebastian's play at the theater. Doris had left a ticket for me at the box office for the first performance. When she told me she left a ticket for Sam also, I had decided to not go. I told her I was too busy packing and I would see the play another weekend. Evidently my defection had not been forgiven. I spent a miserable evening wandering around my silent apartment, washed a load of laundry so I would have clean clothes to take back with me, fixed myself a peanut butter sandwich with a glass of milk, and went to bed.

I awoke in the early hours of the morning to a wet tongue frantically licking the side of my face. Digger was home. He put his head on the pillow next to me and I fell back to sleep to the sound of his gentle snores.

Chapter 14

I was seated at the kitchen table having my morning tea when the intercom buzzed. I carefully stepped over Digger, who was lying at my feet, and hurried to answer it.

I heard, "Kate, can I come up and talk to you about something?"

It was Mira, Sam's daughter.

I buzzed her in and opened the door to my apartment.

She gave me a big hug. "Kate, it's lovely to see you."

"Mira, I didn't know you were in town."

"I'm just here for the weekend. I need some advice about my wedding."

I had met Mira a few months ago when Sam and I had started dating.

"You've set a definite date then?"

"Yes."

Mira was a beautiful, vivacious woman, but today she looked miserable. Even her glorious red hair was lacking its usual bounce.

"What advice do you need? Is it Kevin?"

She sighed. "No, it's my mom."

Sam and Mira's mother had divorced over twenty years ago. Sam's ex-wife remarried and now lived in Cincinnati. Mira worked there in the state attorney general's office. She had met Kevin a couple of years ago when she was in Shelbyville visiting her father.

She sat down on the couch and I waited for the onslaught. It wasn't long in coming. She took a deep breath and everything came pouring out.

"We're fighting about almost everything to do with the wedding. Kevin and I want it held in Shelbyville because that's where most of our friends are. Mom wants it to be in Cincinnati. She wants a big formal affair and thinks my step-father's daughters should be my bridesmaids."

"Kate," she said desperately, "we're not that close. We get along well enough but they're older than me and I only see them on family occasions with my step-father. I don't want a fancy dinner with champagne and an orchestra. I want a wedding that we can enjoy. Maybe a buffet, open bar, or beer and wine, with a DJ so everyone can dance."

She sighed. "The worst thing is she thinks my step-father should walk me down the aisle. That's what we're arguing about the most. She says he raised me. He's a great guy and I'm fond of him but he's not my father. I'm about ready to elope except it would hurt Dad not to be at my wedding. Kate, what am I to do? I know this wedding is a big thing for my mother but it's my wedding, not hers. Shouldn't I be able to have the ceremony I want?"

She looked as if she were ready to cry.

I thought back to my daughter Ellie's wedding. I had wanted it to be perfect with a church full of flowers, a reception at the country club with a formal dinner, beautiful table decorations, champagne fountains and live music. We ended up with a rather scaled down version of the original plan because the groom's mother's theology didn't allow for 'vain show' as she phrased it. She also wanted the whole wedding to be alcohol free but that was a step too far.

We ended up with a dry, rehearsal dinner. Though by the size of the bar bill Jack and I paid, everyone more than made up for this at the country club post-wedding reception.

"Mira, what does your step-dad think about this?"

"I don't know. He's kind of staying out of it."

"Why don't you talk to him? If he's as great a guy as you say maybe he could approach your mother for you. And though he can't walk you down the aisle you could find some other way to acknowledge him in the ceremony. Remember, you are your mother's only child. That's why she wants this wedding to be perfect—she'll only get one shot at it. Maybe you could compromise on some things. You could let her choose the wedding cake or table decorations or decorate the church for the ceremony, hire the photographer—something like that."

Her face cleared. "You think that would work?"

"I'm sure of it."

She jumped up and hugged me. "Kate, thanks for listening, you're the greatest. I'm pretty sure my step-dad will see my side of things and Mom will eventually listens to him. This was turning out to be a miserable weekend, but I feel a lot better now I've talked to you."

"Why miserable?"

"Haven't you heard? There's been another murder—well, attempted murder—the man's not dead but Kevin and Dad are stuck at the hospital in case he regains consciousness."

"A second murder? Who is it?"

Mira shook her head. "I don't know anything yet. All I know is they were called in to the precinct. You know how close-mouthed Dad is, but I'll get it out of Kevin tonight—that's if he ever gets home. And Kate, about Dad…"

"Mira," I said warningly, "your father and I have agreed to end our relationship. It's over."

She interjected, "Dad can be a complete idiot sometimes. You'll work things out."

I shook my head. "Not this time, Mira; we're done. He's moved on and so have I."

"Dad hasn't moved on. He's miserable. I told him he should apologize to you for being such a jerk. But he says you don't want to talk and every time he tries he makes things worse."

I sighed, "Let it go, Mira. It's for the best."

My front door opened abruptly and Doris rushed in. "Kate, I'm glad you're home."

She saw Mira and gave her a big hug. "I didn't know you were here. Stay and eat with us."

"I have to leave, Doris. I'm having lunch with Martha. I'll go out the back way."

Mira disappeared through the kitchen door and I heard her footsteps hurrying down the stairs.

Doris turned to me. "Kate, I'm sorry I wasn't here last night. There was an emergency at the theater. Everyone was supposed to know that Margaret and me takes care of the costumes, but one of the cast took hers home and tried to wash it. She ruined it. We had to go in early to make a last minute replacement otherwise I'd have been here."

"That's okay. At least I had Digger."

"But I wanted to fix a special dinner for your first night back."

She looked upset so I kissed her wrinkled cheek. "You're here now and we'll have a nice cup of tea together."

"What did Mira want?"

"To talk about the wedding; she and her mother are having some issues. And she told me about the other attack."

Doris' mouth dropped open. "What attack?"

I could hardly believe I knew something she didn't, "Hadn't you heard? There was another murder—attempted murder. The guy's in the hospital."

She grabbed my arm. "When did it happen? Do they think it's the same as the other one?"

"That's all I know, Doris. Mira said that Sam and Kevin are at the hospital now."

My intercom buzzed again.

"Mom, it's Ellie."

Doris looked at me in surprise. My daughter, Ellie, never visited unannounced.

"I'd better go. If you hear anything about the attack, let me know—it's important."

And she also left down the back stairs.

Chapter 15

My relationship with my daughter Ellie had been constrained ever since I had divorced her father. Recently, we seemed to be moving closer. I still didn't see enough of her or my two grandsons but at least I saw them on a regular schedule now.

I let her into the apartment and hugged her. "Ellie, what are you doing here this morning? And where are the boys?"

"I left them with Andrew. I wanted to talk to you."

She made her way into the living room and flopped down on the couch.

I studied her face. She looked tense.

"Is everything all right? You seem upset."

She didn't answer me. Instead she asked, "How do you like taking classes?"

Her question surprised me. "I love it. I think I'll double up next semester and take two or even three."

"Have you decided on a major yet?"

"No. It's been a long time since I was in college. There are so many more fields open to women now. I'm going to take classes that I know I'll enjoy and maybe next year I can decide what I want to do." Actually, I was thinking about grad school. I could work on my MLS and then spend time in one of my favorite places, the library.

She sat silent.

"Ellie, what's all this about? Why do you want to talk me?"

She blurted out, "I want to go to college but Andrew is totally opposed to it."

Her eyes filled with tears. "Am I selfish? Am I being a bad mother? The boys will be in kindergarten next year and then full-time school. What am I supposed to do with myself? How did you do it, Mom?"

I decided to tread carefully. "I started college but dropped out when I married your father. He went to law school and I worked until he passed the bar. Then we opened his office here. I ran it up until you were born."

"And then you stayed home full time?"

"Pretty much. That's when we hired Mrs. Carter to do the secretarial work and took on Robert Armstrong as our accountant. After that, I was no longer needed."

"What did you do with yourself?"

"I filled my time with clubs and hobbies, collected antiques, got involved with your school and activities, but it really wasn't enough. I wish I'd started taking classes years earlier."

"Why didn't you?"

"I don't really know. It wasn't something women did then."

"Was Dad opposed to it?"

"We never discussed it. I don't know what he would have thought."

After high school graduation, Ellie had adamantly refused to go to college. Instead, she married Andrew and a year later, the twins were born. Up until now she seemed perfectly content with her role of stay-at-home wife and mother. I wondered what had happened to change her mind.

"Well, I'm going to start school next semester no matter what Andrew says."

"Why doesn't he want you to go?"

"He thinks I'll neglect the boys. I told him I could take classes on Saturdays so he could be home with the children but he wouldn't hear of it—that's his golf day. He's already told me that I shouldn't do it."

"You mean forbidden it?"

"Pretty much."

I could feel the anger starting to churn. Andrew and I didn't have the best relationship. He was five years older than Ellie, the same age difference as that between Jack and me. He had a somewhat rigid personality and I knew he thought my going back to school was ridiculous. I hadn't asked his opinion and he hadn't given it. He didn't need to—his attitude was enough.

"How important is it to you, Ellie?"

"Very."

"What if Andrew stays opposed?"

"I'm still going to do it. What I wanted to ask…" She broke off.

I waited.

"The thing is I might need child care. Have you any ideas?"

"Let me think about it. I'll help when I can. Have you talked to your father about any of this?"

Her mouth tightened. "No, I doubt he'd be much help."

I was surprised. Jack had been a lousy husband but he and Ellie had always been close and he was a doting grandfather. I didn't ask what was wrong between them. Ellie would tell me when she was ready.

"Ellie, to begin with, you could start slowly and just take one or two classes—find something that would fit in with the boys' school schedule. Doris loves the twins. She would be a great baby sitter. I'd pitch in whenever I could and …" I thought of Margaret who always needed something to supplement her meager income, and Frank who had more energy than tasks to fill his day. "I know more people who could help out when Doris wasn't available."

"Do you think Doris would do it?"

"Let's ask her. When I'm through with my summer class I'll invite Doris and a couple of other people I know over to lunch. You can bring the boys to see how they all get along. What about Andrew's mother?"

"She's fond of them but they're too much for her to handle. And I'm not sure how she would feel about my going back to school. She's a little on the traditional side."

A little traditional didn't even come close. There was a long list of things the woman didn't approve of. Shorts, trousers on women, two-piece swimsuits, tattoos and piercings—not that Ellie would consider either one—alcohol, movies, rock music and Harry Potter books. The woman was exhausting to be around. I constantly had to edit my conversation for fear of offending her. Not that I saw her that much. Doris and I had invited her over for an afternoon tea where she had voiced her feelings against divorce and gay marriage. I thought Doris was going to explode and I had to firmly change the direction of the conversation. The visit abruptly ended when Enid and Rose stopped in on their way to a Gay Pride event. Our horrified visitor could hardly get out the door fast enough. The four of us laughed so hard at her retreating back my stomach ached for a week. Dottie, as Andrew's mother was aptly named, hadn't been back since. And needless to say, there was no return invitation.

"Ellie, apart from this, everything else is all right between you and Andrew?"

"Yes, but…"

"But?"

She refused to meet my eyes. "I was talking to Grandma…"

My mother lived in Florida. She and my father had divorced after Jack and I were wed and Mom had married our widowed, family dentist. I always felt she had never quite forgiven me for dropping out of college and Jack was not a favorite of hers—pompous ass, was about the nicest thing she said about him—so we saw each other infrequently. I was surprised that she and Ellie were in contact and said so.

"Grandma called me after you finally told her that you and Dad were divorced. She wanted to know how you were coping. Now she calls regularly. I asked her about going back to school and she encouraged me to give it a try. She said a woman should always be able to take care of herself and being the perfect wife and mother is highly over rated."

That sounded like Mom. I studied Ellie's strained expression. "You'd tell me if something were wrong, wouldn't you?"

She gave an exasperated shake of her head. "Mom, it's just that you and Dad seemed to have the perfect marriage until he had that stupid affair. I don't want to be blind-sided like you were."

"Do you have any reason to think Andrew is cheating on you?"

"No, I guess I'm being pro-active. If anything did happen to my marriage, I'd like to think I would be able to take care of myself and the boys."

I still wasn't convinced, but looking at Ellie's mutinous face, decided to let it go for now.

Chapter 16

The door opened. Doris stuck her head in. "Is she gone?"

I answered in the affirmative.

"She was here a long time."

"She needed to talk to me about something."

"Oh?" This said in an enquiring tone.

I could have kept her on tenterhooks but she'd find out eventually. I'm not sure how she did it but somehow she always knew everything. I stopped teasing her and shared the gist of Ellie's visit.

"You suppose she suspects her husband might be having an affair?"

I thought about that for a minute. "I don't know. She says not, but Andrew's father is a serial philanderer; my mother is divorced. My sister has been divorced twice. I'm divorced. All of us had cheating husbands. Not a record to inspire much confidence in the institution."

"You really think she'd let me babysit the boys?"

"I do. Andrew might raise some objections. He doesn't even like them being around me, but at this point, I don't think Ellie cares what he thinks."

"Kate, why don't you come to our play tonight? Then you can go backstage and see everyone. They're all wondering why you haven't been. There's another thing…" She stopped and took a big breath. "Sam's going to be there."

She saw my face. "Kate, wait one minute. He won't be sitting anywhere near you. I want you to find out something for me. I can't ask him myself. This other murder—well, attempted murder—when did it happen? That's what I need to know. Do you think you could find out? I wouldn't ask if it wasn't important. I'll tell you everything as soon as I can. I promise, Kate."

Talking to Sam was the last thing I wanted to do but I couldn't resist her pleading face. I cautioned her. "You know, Doris, Sam may not want to talk to me."

"He'll talk to you," she said briskly, "and don't forget to ask about the M.O."

"The what?"

"The modus thing—you know—the way the murderer did it." Doris was an avid watcher of crime shows.

"Now come on downstairs. I have a lovely lunch fixed for us."

It felt strange to be sitting in the audience watching my friends instead of being up on stage with them. Sam was sitting two rows in front of me. I could hardly miss those broad shoulders and silver hair. I was devising some strategy to bump into him but I needn't have bothered. I walked out at intermission to get a drink and found him right behind me in the line.

He touched me lightly on the shoulder to get my attention. "Kate?"

I tried to act surprised. "Sam, I didn't expect to see you here. Haven't you another murder to solve?"

"Attempted murder. Yes, I…"

"When did this one happen?"

Surprisingly, he told me. "Sometime Friday morning."

"Was it the same as the other one, the body in the barn?"

"We think so."

That was all I needed to know. I picked up my drink and walked away.

After curtain call, as the chattering audience slowly wended its way out of the theater, I made my way through the crowd and slipped through the backstage door at the side of the auditorium. I hurried toward the women's dressing room, trying not to trip over cables and scenery braces.

"Kate."

It was Sam. He had come through the same door I had.

"Do you have a minute?"

Before I could answer, Pamela Moore came out of the dressing room.

"Sam." She rushed over to him, totally ignoring me, "Did you enjoy the show? I'm so glad you were able to come."

She turned slightly. "Hello, Kate, how are you?" Then she turned back to Sam without waiting for an answer. From the way she was hanging onto his arm, she couldn't have been more obviously staking her claim.

I walked away. I'd almost reached the dressing room door when I felt Sam's hand on my shoulder.

"Kate, I need to talk to you about something."

I looked up at him. His ears were red and he stuttered slightly as if it were hard to get the words out. Pamela was hovering anxiously in the background. If he were about to confess that he and Pamela were in a relationship, I didn't want to hear it.

Doris saved me. She came out of the dressing room. "Kate, everyone's waiting for you. We've got a party to go to at Sebastian's house."

Then she noticed Sam. She bristled, grabbed my arm and almost dragged me away without saying one word to him.

As soon as we were out of earshot, I asked, "Why are you mad at Sam?"

She gave one of her sniffs. "The man's a complete idiot."

Before I could ask what he had done, everyone was there. Enid, Rose, Sebastian, Frank, Margaret, Sylvia and all the rest of the crew crowded around me.

"Kate, you're back."

"How long are you staying?"

"We've missed you so much."

I was carried off to the party on a tidal wave of hugs and kisses. I felt as if I were finally home.

Chapter 17

I was sitting in the diner on the square, waiting for Rose. Doris and Enid had already left for the Sunday matinee. I had packed the car for the drive back to Bloomington so Rose and I agreed we should take separate cars and I would leave from the diner. The party at Sebastian's had gone on until the early hours and we were all moving a little slowly today.

I was hungry. I'd missed breakfast because I got up too late. I was wondering if it would be rude to go ahead and order before Rose arrived, when the door opened and Sam came in. I tried to shrink into myself and become unobtrusive but he saw me right away, almost as if he had been looking for me, and came over to the table.

"Kate, I need to talk to you. Do you mind if I join you?"

"I'm waiting for someone, Sam. They should be here soon."

He sat down opposite me. "I won't take up much of your time. I have a question for you." A pulse in his jaw throbbed.

It didn't look as if I could avoid listening to whatever he wanted to tell me. "Go ahead. Ask away."

"Mira said you told her that I had moved on. What did you mean by that?"

I almost laughed. "Isn't it obvious?"

He leaned across the table. His eyes blazed into mine. "It's not obvious to me. How have I moved on?"

I leaned forward also. "Two words, Sam. Pamela Moore."

His face flushed scarlet, from his chin to his hairline. I thought he was going to choke. "Pamela…"

A voice broke into our conversation. "Kate, I'm sorry to have kept you waiting. Doris asked me to drop off something at the theater. That's why I'm late."

It was Rose. She stood over us and looked from one face to the other with dawning comprehension. "I'll come back later."

I grabbed her arm. "No need, we're done. Detective Williamson was just leaving."

He glared at me. "For now, Kate. Just for now."

Chapter 18

I was in the bottom of our pit working on a patch of stained earth which could have been the remains of a post-hole, but, as I was digging down deeper, was turning out to be nothing more than a tree root, when a shadow fell across me.

I wiped the sweat out of my eyes with my grubby shirt sleeve and looked up to see Adrian looming over me from the top of the excavation. He grinned at me. I had the feeling that I had just smeared dirt all over my face.

"Want to go to dinner with me tonight, Kate?"

That was unexpected. "I..um… with you? Tonight? Well, I don't know…sure."

He gave me that devastating smile. "Can we meet downstairs in the lobby at six-thirty?"

I almost stuttered. "Absolutely, I mean, yes, tonight at six-thirty."

He flashed that smile again. "Great, see you then." Then he quickly left.

I sat back on my heels, mentally kicking myself for sounding like an idiot. Why couldn't I have smiled back and said something like, *I'd love to go to dinner,* or, *that would be great.* No, I had to sound like some freshman being asked out by the captain of the football team. *Grow up,* I told myself. Then I had another thought: How would Cynthia take this? When it came to Adrian she was definitely possessive. Oh well, she could hardly dislike me more than she already did.

The day went well. We were definitely outlining the boundaries of the settlement. Leslie unearthed more pottery fragments and Greg was delirious over getting the chance to reconstruct not only the pot I had unearthed, but a second one with a differing design.

"Each family decorated their pottery in their own unique way. Look how different this one is." He reverently ran his fingers across the tracings painted into the surface.

I smiled. Greg's hands were moving, almost shaping the outline of the earthenware vessel he was envisioning. "When will you start on it?"

"Not until we've finished up here and have everything back in the lab. But Wendell has promised that it can be my project."

The rest of my team would be in IU-Bloomington for the fall semester. I would be in Indianapolis so I would miss all the lab work.

"Why so sad, Kate?"

I looked up again. This time it was Dusty.

"When everything we've found goes back to the lab for processing, I'll be in Shelbyville. So I'll miss out on the most important part."

He laughed. "You can always drive down and visit. Don't worry; we'll be digging here for at least one more season. Maybe you'll sign up next year."

"I can do that. Will you be here next year?"

His face fell. Until then he had been smiling. "I don't know, Kate. I just don't know."

I immediately wished I could take the question back. Why did I have to remind him why he was working in Bloomington instead of Belize?

He walked away, shoulders slumped, the picture of dejection. Here I was feeling sorry for myself because Sam had dumped me for somebody else, which was mostly my fault because I was the one who had originally dumped him. Dusty had a wife and child that he loved but was separated from because some crazy person was stalking him.

Bracing myself, I picked up my bucket of dirt, swung it up on top of the screen and started sifting. There was nothing like hard work for clearing the mind and setting priorities such as, I needed to pass this class.

During lunch break, Sal and I were sharing a patch of shade when she suddenly asked, "What did you say to Wendell that upset him?"

I didn't think anyone had noticed us talking. "I asked him if he was going to run the dig next season."

"What did he say?"

"That he didn't know."

She thought about that then opened her mouth to ask something else.

I wanted to change the thread of the conversation so I quickly interjected,

"Sal, Adrian invited me to dinner tonight. It took me by surprise so I said yes. Now I'm wondering if I should have accepted."

She started to laugh. "Go. Adrian is a nice guy. You'll have fun. It's good to get away once in a while."

I thought for a moment. "What I really want to say is, I'm a little concerned about Cynthia. Is there anything I should know about their relationship?"

"Honey, there is no relationship. I don't know if you've noticed, but Adrian doesn't exactly bat for our team."

My mouth dropped open. "You mean he's gay?"

"One hundred per cent." She laughed. "Cynthia refuses to accept it. I don't know if she thinks she can convert him to our side. Poor Adrian is always trying to avoid her, which is darn near impossible when we work and live so close to each other."

I didn't know how to respond to that and ended up with a bemused, "Oh."

Chapter 19

Adrian looked gorgeous in a green silk shirt that matched his eyes, and a pair of casual cream-colored slacks. As we walked to the restaurant, I noticed heads turning, not all of them women.

I had brought mostly work clothes but managed to dig out a long skirt and colorful top from the bottom of my suitcase.

"You look beautiful tonight, Kate."

I almost said, *you look beautiful too*, but stopped myself just in time. Instead I muttered a brief, *thank you.*

Adrian had chosen a Mexican restaurant, a block from campus. It was crowded but there was no one there I recognized.

He leaned over the table and smiled at me, "Margarita, Kate?"

"Sure." I looked around. The dining room was bright and cheerful, filled with succulent plants overflowing their colorful pots. A mariachi band played in the background, the chairs were comfortable and the food smelled wonderful. I sipped my margarita, relaxed and started to enjoy the evening.

"So tell me a little something about yourself. I know you're divorced after a long marriage…" He stopped with a wry grin on his face. "Oops, I wasn't supposed to say that."

I frowned. "What else do you know about me?"

He looked deep into my eyes. "I know that you and Dusty dated through high school but broke up when he started college, that you were divorced after thirty years of marriage, that you attacked your husband with one of his own golf clubs when you caught him in a compromising position with his secretary, and that it probably wouldn't be a good idea to make you angry."

"And because of that you asked me out to dinner?"

He put his elbows on the table and rested his chin on his clasped hands. "I asked you out because you're a very attractive woman and I wanted to get to know you better."

I couldn't find fault with that. "How do you know so much about me?"

"Dusty and I were at college together in Arizona. You guys had just broken up and he talked about you a lot. When you signed up for this dig, he briefly wondered about your motive then accepted your explanation that you hadn't realized he was the professor in charge."

"That was true, Adrian."

"I know. I've watched you and you've been careful to not reveal that you and Dusty knew each other prior to this."

"Then you know about his...?"

"Stalker? Yes. I hope it's resolved soon. It's tearing him up to be separated from Sheila and Lily."

I sighed. "I can only imagine."

He put his hand over mine. "Let's forget about that for this evening. I do want to get to know you better. Are you seeing anyone?"

"Not really," I said reluctantly. I don't know why I didn't answer, "no." It was hard to accept that Sam and I were through. It was as if by acknowledging it, I would make it real.

"Is that a yes or no?"

"It's a no. I'm pretty certain it's over. He's already found someone else."

He squeezed my hand. "His loss, my gain." He picked up the menu. "Let's order."

Later, as we were walking back to the dorm, Adrian took my hand. "Next time we go out on a date you're going to let me pay."

My dating guru, Sylvia had drummed into me her three rules of dating. Always drive your own car. Never meet your date at your house. And always pay your own way.

"But Adrian, this wasn't a date. I expected to pay for myself."

He stopped, put his hands on my shoulders and looked down at me, eyes twinkling. "I was under the impression this was a date."

I didn't know how to answer that so we walked the rest of the way back to the dorm in silence.

When we stopped on the landing that divided the male and female dorms he put his arms around me and held me close. "Kate, I enjoyed this evening. Can we do it again?"

Before I could answer, he leaned down and kissed me full on the lips, then quickly left. I stood for a moment, too shocked to move. When I recovered and started to walk down the hallway back to my room, I heard a door quietly close.

The next morning, I ran into Sal on my way to the dining hall.

"Hi, Kate. How did your date go?"

"It wasn't a date. Adrian and I just had dinner together."

She laughed. "Tell that to Cynthia. She had a face like a thundercloud when I saw her in the bathroom this morning."

My heart sank. Cynthia and I were never going to be friends but I wanted to avoid any open hostility. As we walked into the dining hall I saw that she was sitting at a table with Adrian. Greg, Dawna and Leslie were on the opposite side of the room.

"I'm going to sit with my team, Sal."

"Wise choice," she chuckled.

So I did.

Chapter 20

"Why are you avoiding me?"

Adrian squatted down on the side of our excavation. I looked around. Greg was screening dirt a few yards away. Dawna had gone to the bus at the side of the field to refill her water bottle from the cooler. Leslie was taking the bags with our finds to the tent set up in the shade at the side of the field. I was trapped.

I decided for honesty. "I think Cynthia knows that we went to dinner together. She's barely speaking to me and I want to avoid a confrontation."

He frowned. "So are you saying that Cynthia dictates who we see and what we do? That's giving her a lot of power."

I shrugged my shoulders. "Adrian, I want to pass the course."

"And you think Cynthia might sabotage your grade?"

"I don't know but I'd rather not risk it."

"You're worrying about nothing. All four of us, Wendell, Sal, Cynthia and me decide on grades. You'll receive the grade you've earned."

"I wish I could be as sure of that as you seem to be."

"Tell you what," he jumped down into the pit, hunkered down next to me and spoke quietly in my ear, "I'll be in Shelbyville this weekend with Dusty. Can we have dinner there?"

I thought about it for a moment. It was the closing weekend of the play. Everyone would be at the theater and I would be alone again. "I'd like that. Give me a call and we can arrange to meet somewhere."

He flashed a smile at me and hurriedly left. I looked up. Cynthia stood at the screening table with Greg. He handed her a shard of pottery and looked as if he were explaining something to her. Instead of listening to him, she was scowling at me. Abruptly, she turned and strode after Adrian, leaving Greg with his mouth hanging open mid-sentence.

Something strange happened later that morning. I had gone to use the—what Doris called "facilities"—which were two rather odiferous Porta-Potties. I avoided them as much as possible not because of the smell—you got used to that after a couple of days—but because of the heat. The temperatures were in the nineties and the Porta-Potties were standing in full sun. Nobody lingered inside because it was so hot it felt like a sauna.

I could feel the sweat trickling down my back almost as soon as I closed the door. I hurried, not wanting to spend a second longer in there than needed. The handle was hot to my touch and I quickly turned it to exit the place but the door didn't open. I pushed but it wouldn't budge. Kicking didn't work either. It was thoroughly jammed.

Finally, I yelled for help, "The door won't open! I can't get out!"

I listened. Only silence. I tried shouting again—this time a lot louder—but still no response. I tried not to panic. On my walk over I hadn't seen anyone at this end of the field. Yelling again produced nothing. It seemed as if the temperature had risen in the short time I'd been trapped in there. It had to be at least a hundred and twenty now. How long before dehydration set in? Again, I yelled but nobody answered. Just as I was about to give up, I heard a tentative voice.

"Are you all right in there?"

"No, I can't open the door."

I heard a scraping sound, the door slowly swung open and I saw Greg's bewildered face. He was holding a sturdy branch in his hand.

For a moment we stood there staring at each other in puzzlement. Then he handed it to me. "This is what jammed the door. It was pushed through the handle."

I stumbled out into the relatively cool air and took some deep breaths. Was it just a sick joke or something more?

It had been an uncomfortable week. I did my best to avoid Cynthia, which didn't work. I ran into her in the shared bathroom, the dining hall, on the stairs and passing her room. She didn't acknowledge me in any way and I ignored her.

I was glad to be going home for the weekend. It would be a welcome break from her unrelenting hostility. Traffic was heavy and it was late afternoon before I got back to Shelbyville.

Doris had cooked a great meal, and Rose, Enid and I went down to eat with her. When they all left for the theater, I sat on the couch with Digger at my feet, and flipped through a few magazines before deciding to go into the den to see if there was anything on television that would be worth watching.

As I passed the front door, my intercom buzzed. It was Sam.

"Can I come up and talk to you for a few moments?"

I buzzed him in because I couldn't think of an excuse not to and within a minute he was at my apartment door.

"What do you want, Sam?"

He stood in the doorway. The tips of his ears were red but he was otherwise calm. "We never finished our conversation at the diner last weekend."

I led the way into the living room and sat in one of the armchairs. I didn't want him sitting next to me on the couch.

"What did you want to add?"

He cleared his throat nervously. "You seem to think there's some kind of relationship between Pamela Moore and me."

"She seems to think there is, too. Besides I've seen you together. Two days after we broke up the last time you met her for dinner at Luigi's."

A pulse started throbbing in his jaw. "I have never met Pamela Moore for dinner anywhere."

"I saw you, Sam. Going into Luigi's together, then at the auditions for the play, at the diner, and last weekend at the theater when she was hanging all over you."

A red-faced Sam almost yelled, "I'm telling you the truth."

Digger scrambled to his feet and rushed for the kitchen. He hated confrontation. I heard the flap of his doggy door as he left for more congenial company.

"Why should I believe you? I told you the truth about not knowing Dusty was running the dig and you called me a liar and stormed out of the diner. How does it feel, Sam?"

By now we were on our feet glaring at each other. I saw him take a deep breath and fight for control. "I'm sorry; I may have made a mistake."

"May have? What is it, you can't admit to making a mistake or you still think I lied to you?"

"Whenever I try to make things right between us you find something else to be mad about." He ground the words out through clenched teeth.

"Just leave. You know where the door is." I walked out of the room. There was silence. Then I heard footsteps and the sound of my front door slamming shut.

Chapter 21

"Kate, would you have time to drive me to the grocery store?"

Doris and I were seated at the kitchen table. We had just finished one of her lavish breakfasts and Digger was lying at my feet on the alert for any crumbs that might fall his way.

"Of course I would. I have no plans before dinner tonight."

"Where are you eating?"

"Luigi's. Where else?"

"Are you meeting anyone?"

Doris really wanted to know if I were meeting Sam.

"I'm meeting one of the instructors on the dig. He's in town this weekend."

"Oh."

I could see she wanted to ask more questions so I quickly told her that I'd come down to her apartment as soon as I finished cleaning up the kitchen. I loaded the dishwasher, kissed Digger goodbye and was rewarded with one of his sloppy dog licks. Doris was already waiting for me at her back door.

"Kate, I have to go over to Mrs. Turner's place. She wants me to return her library books and she might need something from the grocery store."

Mrs. Turner was a shut-in who lived in a small cottage on the alley, opposite our house. She was also our neighborhood watch coordinator, a position she took very seriously. As Sam had told me in the days when we were actually speaking to each other, Mrs.

Turner called the police dispatcher for the slightest infraction. If someone parked on the alley, a suspicious-looking person passed by, a neighbor made too much noise, or if she even suspected underage drinking, or drug use, the police department got a call.

In return, since she was rarely able to leave her home, we did favors and ran errands for her. Getting in and out of her house was never easy. She had few visitors and liked to chat with anyone who came to call. This time she wanted to know all about the dig.

"Can you get me books on native Americans in Indiana, especially Shelby County? What you're doing sounds interesting. And to think they were living here almost a thousand years ago."

I promised her I would. Her shopping list took some time and I could see Doris anxiously checking her watch. She had to be at the theater in a couple of hours.

We cut our library visit short. Sylvia, Sebastian and Frank weren't there and I was able to escape from Clarice, our self-designated head volunteer, by promising to meet her for breakfast after I was finished with the dig. The grocery store wasn't full and we finished our shopping in record time.

"Just one more stop to pick up some chickens at the butcher's. Then we're done."

I would have been content with meat from the grocery store but Doris insisted on going to the local butcher shop. "Farm raised, it's the only way to go," she said, setting her mouth, "I like to know where it comes from."

The problem was that Doris and the butcher had a running feud. Since she and her late husband had raised hogs and cattle on their farm, she had extremely high standards when it came to choosing the cuts of meat and having them trimmed to her exact specifications.

To my surprise, she picked out what she wanted from the display case with no special requests. The butcher wrapped them and waited for more.

"I need ten chickens cut up." She turned to me, "We're having a fried chicken dinner at the senior center." She sounded almost apologetic.

He glared at her. He really was an unpleasant man.

"Ada."

His wife came in from the back room. She was a tiny little woman and the plastic apron she wore over her white smock hung almost to her feet.

"She," he jerked his thumb back at Doris, "wants ten chickens cut up."

Ada gave us an apologetic smile and left. I could hear the thud of her cleaver as she worked on the poultry Doris had ordered. She returned a few minutes later with a large parcel wrapped in butchers' paper and tied with twine.

"I wrapped all the different parts separately for you."

We thanked her and left.

As we got into the car, I said, "The butcher was pretty rude today. I'm surprised you didn't say something."

She sighed. "I may have been too hard on him. You know their shop is called Fletcher and Son? Well, there isn't a son any more. Mrs. Turner told me he was killed in a car accident about three months ago. He was driving drunk and ran off the road. He hit a tree and broke his neck."

I didn't ask any more questions. We dropped the groceries and books off at Mrs. Turner's house and only escaped when Doris promised to visit her once the show was over and she had more free time. I carried the bags in for Doris and would have helped her put everything away but she ushered me to the door, saying, "Thanks for taking me. I can handle things from here."

By which I figured Doris didn't want me in her apartment and I was left to wonder why.

Chapter 22

I took extra care getting ready for my dinner date with Adrian that evening. He usually saw me in dusty jeans and mud-stained shirts, and for once I wanted him to see me dressed up.

We had arranged to meet at seven and Adrian, Dusty and I arrived at Luigi's parking lot at the same time. The cream linen sheath dress I chose to wear looked great against my tan and Adrian was suitably impressed.

"Kate, you look absolutely beautiful."

Adrian was gorgeous in black slacks, black silk shirt, and a cream-colored linen jacket. It was almost as if we planned to color coordinate.

The baggy jeans and flannel shirt worn by Dusty was in stark contrast. "Are you eating with us, Dusty?"

He smiled. "No, just dropping Adrian, then I'm going to an internet café to Skype Sheila and Lily. I'll be back in a couple of hours to pick him up."

"I could drop him off, if that's easier for you."

He shook his head. "Better not. You shouldn't be seen anywhere near my sister's house."

I watched him leave and, as Adrian and I turned to mount the steps to Luigi's front door, I saw a flicker of movement on the edge of the parking lot. There was someone standing behind a tall bush. The light was beginning to fade and I couldn't make out who it was.

"Are you coming, Kate?"

I looked again but whoever it was had disappeared so I followed Adrian into the restaurant.

The last time I'd been in Luigi's, Sam and I had argued over my spending the summer in Bloomington. Up until then our relationship had been progressing smoothly and I was beginning to think it might be moving towards something more permanent. It was still hard to accept how quickly it had fallen apart and how quickly Sam had found someone else.

Adrian was looking at me with a quizzical stare., "A penny for them?"

I shook my head. "Not worth it." And I put all thoughts of Sam out of my mind and concentrated on enjoying dinner with Adrian.

The food as always was wonderful. I ordered my favorite seafood fettuccini and our conversation flowed as freely as the wine.

"Kate, when Dusty returns to our dig in Belize, I hope you'll be there with us."

"You describe it so vividly. I almost feel I'm there already."

He leaned across the table. "Belize is a beautiful, romantic place, perfect for lovers." He took my hand and kissed it.

I would have been squirming with embarrassment if I hadn't known he were gay. If he acted the same way with Cynthia it was little wonder she thought they were in a relationship. I almost felt sorry for her. He broke into my thoughts. "Who's that guy staring at you?"

I turned. The bar was directly opposite the dining room. Again, I saw that flicker of movement. It was on the periphery of my vision. I scooted all the way around in my chair but I didn't see anybody.

"No, Kate—over by the door."

Sam was standing to the side of the dining room entrance. He was staring at us both. When he saw me look at him, he dropped his eyes and followed Luigi to a table on the other side of the room. I avoided looking at him but I could still feel his looming presence. I was self conscious every time Adrian held my hand or leaned over and looked deep into my eyes.

"What's wrong?"

Adrian had to repeat himself before I heard him.

"Nothing."

"It's that guy over there who can't stop staring at us, isn't it? Is he your ex?"

There was no point in concealing it. "Yes, we broke up a few weeks ago and it's still a little uncomfortable."

"But definitely ended, right?"

Why did I hate to admit it? Reluctantly I answered, "It's over."

"Kate, darling."

And there, tottering toward us on her ridiculously high heels was the person I disliked most in the world, Bitch Barbara. The woman kept turning up at the most inopportune moments.

"Look at you dining with this handsome man while Sam is glowering at you from across the room." She gave one of her fake giggles. "Introduce me."

"No."

Her eyes opened wide. "What do you mean, no?"

I'd had enough of Bitch Barbara. I was not about to let her ruin my evening. "I mean, no. I won't introduce you. I don't want you here, so go peddle your poison elsewhere."

I heard a snort of laughter from Adrian.

Barbara's mouth dropped open. A dull flush suffused her face. "Why are you being so hateful? I thought we were friends."

"Don't give me your fake outrage. We were never friends. You have no friends."

She opened and closed her mouth, couldn't choke out any words, turned on her heel and tottered away.

I took a hefty swig of wine. "Sorry about that."

Adrian trapped my hand again. "You must really dislike that woman."

"I have my reasons."

"Which are?"

I shook my head and pulled my hand away. "Not now, maybe some other time."

Just then, Dusty came in the back door of the restaurant and saved me from further explanation. He waved at us, but before he could make his way to the table Sam intercepted him. They talked briefly then with a look at us, Dusty followed him back to his table where they sat and entered into an intense conversation. Sam stood, handed Dusty what looked like one of his business cards, strode through the restaurant and, without even glancing at me as he passed our table, exited the front door.

Dusty followed him, a thoughtful look on his face. "Are you ready to go?"

I looked at Adrian. He nodded. We followed Dusty out of the restaurant.

Adrian asked, "Did you talk to…?"

"Yes." Dusty looked happy and more relaxed. It must have been a good Skype visit.

We turned down the side of the building where I had parked. Sam was coming towards us. He was almost sprinting.

"Kate, wait don't go there!"

But he spoke too late. I'd already seen it. My car was sitting at an odd angle and before I even looked at the other side, I knew that all four tires had been slashed.

Chapter 23

Sam immediately took charge. "Kate, I'll take you home. Then we can get the police report. I'll get a tow for the car." He turned away and dialed his cell phone. After a brief conversation, he turned back to us. "Tow truck's on its way. They're going to take it to the police impound yard. I want to take a closer look at it."

Adrian put a comforting arm around my shoulders. "Kate doesn't have to wait around for that, I'll take her home."

Dusty cut him off. "No, Adrian, you and I need to stay away from Kate. Let Detective Williamson take her."

He and Sam exchanged looks. Sam nodded. "I've got people on the way who'll handle this." The words no sooner left his mouth when a couple of unmarked cars entered the lot. Sam walked over to the officers and had a lengthy conversation with them.

He finally turned to me. "Let's go, Kate."

Adrian looked as if he were about to argue so I quickly said, "Goodnight. Thanks for dinner and a wonderful evening."

"I'm sorry it ended this way." He leaned forward, took me in his arms and kissed me. I saw Sam's lips tighten.

Adrian's arm was still around my shoulder. "You'll need a ride back to school, tomorrow."

Dusty interrupted him. "Have some common-sense, man. You know we can't take her. Isn't it enough that her car's been trashed?"

"Sorry, I wasn't thinking."

Sam glared at him then turned to me, "Ready, Kate?"

He was silent on the drive back to the house. Instead of dropping me off at the front door, he drove around to the alley and parked.

"I need to get some information from you. Do you mind if I come in?"

I led the way into the living room and collapsed into a chair. Sam sat opposite me on the couch. He leaned forward. "Do you have any idea who would have done this to your car?"

My head was throbbing. I tried to ignore it and answer him. "I had an altercation with Barbara Armstrong this evening."

"About what?"

"She came over to my table and asked to be introduced to Adrian. I said no."

"Just no?"

"Well, there was a little more to it than that. I told her to go peddle her poison elsewhere."

I saw Sam's mouth twitch. "What was her reaction?"

"She acted hurt and I do mean acted. She said she thought we were friends and I told her we weren't."

"So it's fair to say that she was upset or angry?"

I sighed. "Yes."

"Anyone else?"

"I thought I saw someone in the parking lot, and later in the bar I felt someone watching me. I couldn't see who it was. Maybe I imagined it."

"You say this person was in the bar?"

"Yes."

Sam got up and paced the floor for a moment, thinking. He turned back to me.

"What about people on the dig? Anyone there raise a red flag?"

"There's Cynthia. She's one of the team leaders. She doesn't like me."

"Any particular reason?"

"She has a thing about Adrian and she acts as if she's jealous of me, which is stupid because…"

"Why is it stupid? Aren't you and Adrian dating?"

"I wouldn't exactly call it dating. We went to dinner last week and Cynthia found out. She's been even more unfriendly since then. I told Adrian I didn't want to go out with him again."

Sam gave me one of his piercing looks. "Because?"

"Cynthia will be grading my work and I want to pass the class."

"You said it was stupid. Why?"

"Adrian is gay."

He pursed his lips. "Are you sure about that? He sure doesn't act gay."

"Yes. Sal told me and she's known him a long time."

"Who's Sal?"

"Another team leader. She's worked with Dusty for years."

"Anyone else who's worked with him before?"

I thought for a moment. "Two of the people on my team, Dawna and Leslie, have been on digs with him in Belize. I don't know about the other students."

He sat back on the couch. "Tomorrow, Kate, I'll take you back to Bloomington."

"You don't have to do that, Sam. I can rent a car."

He shook his head. "That's not a good idea. If you rented a car, the same thing might happen down at IU. Or it could be something that wouldn't show up until you were on the road. Let me take you, please."

I was too tired to argue. "All right."

He looked relieved.

"Just one more thing, Sam. How is the murder investigation coming along?"

For a moment he hesitated then answered me. "It's stalled for the moment. There's nothing new on the body in the barn. The other victim is unconscious. We can't question him and we still can't find Stephen Wills." He stood up, swaying slightly.

"Sam, are you sure you should be driving."

He sat down abruptly and gave a wry grin. "Is that an invitation?"

I turned away so he couldn't see the blood rush to my face. "I just meant that if you want to bed down in the den, you're welcome to it. After all, you're my ride tomorrow."

"Thanks, I'm a little sleep deprived right now, but I'd better go back to my place."

"Suit yourself."

I walked into the kitchen to let Sam out the back door and stood there waiting until I realized he hadn't followed me. I came back into the living room to find out what was keeping him. His head was slumped on the back of the couch, his mouth slightly open and he was softly snoring. Carefully, I took off his shoes, slid his legs up on the couch and placed a pillow under his head. As I leaned forward to cover him with a quilt, he rolled over and his arms enfolded me. For a moment I stayed there feeling the warmth of him and his soft breath against my cheek. He murmured something, his arms slackened and dropped away. I tucked the quilt around him and gently stroked his face. I really missed Sam.

Chapter 24

"Kate, aren't you up yet?"

I wanted to say—*does it look like I'm up?*—but it was too early to indulge in witty repartee. I sat up in bed and pushed the hair out of my eyes. "What time is it, Doris?"

"Almost ten-thirty; you slept late. I've fed Digger and I'm leaving for the theater. I wanted to say goodbye."

I scrambled out of bed and gave her a hug. We walked together to the kitchen and she put the kettle on for tea. "I've got time for a quick cup but Margaret and I want to get in early so we can get the costumes collected before everyone gets there."

The play had closed the previous night and today the whole cast and crew would be at the theater breaking down the set and storing the flats and props.

I gathered the mugs and teabags and had my head in the refrigerator looking for the milk when I heard a surprised Doris say, "Sam, I didn't know you spent the night?"

My head came out so fast I hit it on the side of the door. Sam was standing in the doorway clad only in a t-shirt and pair of boxer shorts. He gave us a startled look. "Excuse me." And he hurriedly left the room.

Doris turned on the coffee pot and got another mug out of the cabinet. She was beaming.

He came back, more suitably dressed this time. "Sorry. I didn't realize anyone was up yet."

He looked at Doris. "Kate's car was vandalized last night so I brought her home. By the time we got the police report done, it was late and I fell asleep on the couch."

"Vandalized? Who would do such a thing?"

"That's what we were discussing last night."

"Oh, Kate, that's terrible." She hugged me tightly. "How are you going to get back to school today with no car?"

Before I could answer, Sam said, "I'm going to drive her down and pick her up next Friday, too."

"Sam..."

He raised his hand to stop me. "It's non-negotiable, Kate."

Doris looked at his face. "I'd better get going. I don't think I have time for tea." She hugged me again. "See you next weekend, Kate. Coffee's on Sam." And smiling broadly, she quickly left.

"Sam, you don't have to drive me all the way to Bloomington."

"As I just said, it's non-negotiable." He grinned at me. "Are you going to argue?"

I looked at his broad shoulders, blue eyes and silver hair, spending time with Sam suddenly seemed very attractive. "No, whatever you say."

That surprised him so much, he couldn't think of another word.

We were in the diner having a late breakfast before getting on the road for the trip back to IU. Somehow, Sam's overnight stay on my couch had developed a kind of truce between us. As long as we kept away from the subject of Adrian, we were having a pleasant meal with no arguments.

"So why do you think it's a palisaded village?"

We were talking about the dig and I was explaining the significance of the organic stains. He seemed genuinely interested and I was enjoying myself.

"Sam."

I looked up to see Pamela Moore standing at the side of the table.

"I need to talk to you." She looked at me. "If you don't mind, it's personal."

I wasn't sure what to do. I glanced at Sam. Did he want me to leave?

His face tightened. "Mrs. Moore, I'm off-duty and I'm trying to have a private meal with no interruptions. Go to the station. I'm sure someone there can help you."

She gave him a pleading look. "I would have asked you last night at Luigi's but by the time I got there you were gone." She turned to me. "I hear your new boyfriend is very handsome and that you two looked as if you were enjoying dinner."

I smiled at her. "You're making an assumption, Pamela. He's a work colleague not a boyfriend."

"Why were you looking for me in Luigi's?"

Sam's voice was harsh and Pamela was startled by the question.

She stuttered slightly, "I was going to ask you to the cast party last night. Or if you didn't want to go, I thought we could have dinner together—you almost always eat alone"

"What makes you think I would want to go to a cast party or eat dinner?"

He didn't say, "with you," but his tone definitely implied it.

Pamela reddened. She opened her mouth but Sam cut her off.

"What time were you there?"

"I don't know. A few minutes after the curtain came down."

"So after the show you went straight to Luigi's?"

"No, I changed out of costume first so maybe ten or fifteen minutes later."

Sam spoke dismissively. "That's all the questions for now. If we need you to answer any more we'll do that down at the precinct."

She smiled tremulously, "Right now?"

"No, someone from the station will call you."

He turned to me, smiled and took my hand. "Where were we? You've only got two more weeks on the dig and then you're back for good?"

Pamela stood there for another couple of minutes. We both ignored her and went on with our conversation. I heard the door of the diner slam. "Is she gone?"

"Yes. The woman turns up everywhere. I wish I hadn't..." He stopped.

I took my hand away. "Hadn't what?"

He sighed. "Around the time you and I split up, I ran into her on Luigi's parking lot. She had some questions about whether or not she would be notified if her ex-husband was released from prison. Hell, Kate, I felt sorry for her. You know the kind of man she was married to."

I did. I had dated her ex-husband a couple of times until I found out he had been abusive to her.

Sam went on, "I let her sit at my table while I explained the procedure. Then she wouldn't leave so I ordered my meal to go. I guess that was too subtle for her because since then I run into her everywhere. I was hoping it was coincidence until that night at the theater with you when I realized it wasn't. I swear, Kate, I've done nothing to encourage her."

I giggled, "Do women often find you irresistible?"

"Damn it, Kate, it's not funny. Look at what's happening with Dusty. And what happened to your car. It can be dangerous—not for me but for you."

On the drive to Bloomington, I asked, "Who do you think trashed my car?"

"Someone who hates you. It wasn't just vandalism; there was a lot of rage behind the attack."

He leaned over the console toward me. "You've got to be careful, Kate. Be alert to what's going on around you. Stay in well-lit areas and don't go anywhere alone at night."

I almost said *what are you, my mom?* But it was no time for joking. He was deadly serious.

"I promise, Sam."

He squeezed my hand. "How well do you know Adrian?"

"Not very. He's a fun guy and great to work with. I've had dinner with him a couple of times."

I felt Sam stiffen. "He knows about the stalking and the fact that Dusty is married not divorced. They've known each other since college and worked together over the years." I stopped. "You surely can't suspect Adrian?"

"At this point nobody can be ruled out, except you."

"Sam, how did you get involved in this?"

"I got a call from a detective in Phoenix. He found out I was the officer who arrested you after you attacked your ex-husband and he wanted to check up on you. When I saw Dusty I..." He broke off.

"When you saw Dusty—what?"

"Please don't get angry, Kate. I wanted to know whether he had told you he was still married. I wanted to tell him that no way could you be the stalker. And I needed to know that he hadn't told anyone that you and he had once dated."

I was touched by his concern. "It's all right, Sam. Dusty told me everything. He asked me if I was sure about working on the dig and we both agreed to act as strangers to each other."

Sam relaxed and took my hand again. He didn't release it until an oncoming semi started to veer over into our lane and he needed both hands on the wheel.

"Who's the new man?"

I was standing in front of the dorm watching Sam's SUV disappear into the distance when Cynthia asked the question. The fact that Cynthia was even talking to me took me by surprise so my answer was on the curt side.

"A friend of mine. I had a little car trouble so he drove me here."

She smirked. "You seem to have a lot of men paying court to you."

I smiled back. I was getting really tired of her nonsense. "I do, don't I?" She staggered slightly as I pushed past her to greet Dawna who had arrived just ahead of me.

That evening at dinner, Dawna was the only member of my team in the dining room. Greg and Leslie weren't back from their weekend yet. I grabbed her by the arm and steered her over to Adrian's table. I was going to enjoy my last two weeks. If that meant Cynthia would try to sabotage my grade, so be it. I wouldn't go down without a fight. I could play dirty too.

Chapter 25

It promised to be an exciting day. Dusty told us to mark every post-hole we had found, with a white, paper plate. We were standing around in our various groups wondering what was going on, when Cynthia passed by.

Dawna and Leslie stopped her. "What's happening? Why the paper plates? We've already charted the post-holes."

I didn't bother asking her anything and, sure enough, she turned her back on me and answered the rest of the team.

"He's going to do some aerial photography." And with that, she walked away.

Sal took pity on us. "Wendell's friend has a crop dusting plane. He's going to take Wendell and then Adrian up with him. They'll photograph the site from the air to get a better view of how it's laid out. That's the reason for the paper plates. If all the post-holes are marked, we can get an aerial view of the location of the dwellings and palisade. If there are any unexplained gaps, they might point us in the direction of where we should dig with the time we have left."

"When will we know the results?"

"In a day or two. Exciting huh?"

Dawna, Leslie, Greg and I marked everything in our section, then sat back to watch the plane overhead. It swooped down low over the field and we saw Dusty recording everything with his cameras. The plane made a few more passes over the field then dipped its wings and flew away to a nearby landing strip. Sal told us to pick up the plates and get back to work.

As we were walking towards the dorm after a full day at the site, Sal asked me, "Did you run into Wendell or Adrian over the weekend?"

For a moment I was speechless then decided honesty was the best policy.

"Adrian and I had dinner together."

She raised an eyebrow.

"Originally, I told him I wouldn't go to dinner with him again because I didn't want any confrontation with Cynthia. It's uncomfortable enough the way it is. He told me he would be in Shelbyville for the weekend and suggested we go to a restaurant there."

It was my turn for questions. "What did you do this weekend?"

"Relaxed and got a lot of reading out of the way. All the kids were off camping in Brown County. Wendell, Adrian and Cynthia were out of town. I had the place to myself."

"Same here except for meeting Adrian. It was the last weekend of the play at our local theater and all my friends were involved in it one way or another, so I was alone."

"What about the guy who dropped you off yesterday? Cynthia seemed to think he was a new boyfriend."

"Cynthia can think whatever she wants. I had car trouble so a friend brought me back."

I was getting irritated by the personal questions, and Sal must have noticed because she left me with a curt, "See you at dinner."

Dawna, Leslie, Greg and I stayed late at the dining hall because Adrian had come over to our table and was entertaining us with funny tales about digs he had participated in. Cynthia had tried to join the conversation but Adrian pointedly ignored her and she moved to another table, where she sat like a brooding Buddha glaring at us. Leslie had a great story about a snake in her sleeping bag and Dawna told us about encountering piranhas in the river she was using as her bath-tub. "I ran out screaming and for the rest of the dig made my ablutions in my tent with a basin of water and a sponge." Greg and I laughed politely but somehow snakes and piranhas didn't seem that funny. We stayed until the dining hall closed and the staff ran us out by clearing the dishes off the table and sweeping the floor under our feet.

The minute I walked into my room, I knew someone had been in there. My clothes were hanging in the closet just as I had left them. Everything on the shelves looked untouched. But I hadn't used the desk or dresser because they smelled musty, yet two of the drawers were slightly open and I knew they had both been closed when I left my room.

My purse was in a slightly different place on top of the desk. I quickly checked it. The cash and credit cards were untouched but my driver's license was in the wrong slot.

I picked up my phone and started to dial Sam's number then cancelled the call. It was late and there was nothing he could do from so far away. Why worry him? Still, it was an unsettling feeling knowing that someone had looked through my personal belongings and now knew where I lived. I checked that the door was securely locked and found the screws on the bolt were almost falling out of their holes. Had they always been like that or did someone loosen them? I tried tightening them with the end of a metal nail file but it wasn't very successful. I ended up jamming the desk chair under the door knob and spent a wakeful night, tossing and turning until the morning sun shone through the blinds.

Another unnerving incident happened that week. Adrian and I were walking back to the dorm from the dining hall. It was dark and no one else was around. Adrian was holding my hand and asking about Sam.

"The ex-boyfriend doesn't seem to know your relationship is over."

I wasn't sure what to say. Adrian was gay but he seemed more and more to be acting like some kind of jealous lover. "Sam and I..."

He stopped and turned to me, "Sam and I what?"

"Adrian, I don't know what our relationship is right now."

And I didn't. Sam and I seemed to be moving closer to each other but we were still a long way from the way we used to be.

"Are you telling me that you're just leading me on? That you and the boyfriend might be getting back together?"

"What do you mean leading you on? We're friends, nothing more."

I didn't understand why he was angry. "Besides, you're gay. Why would you be interested in anything other than friendship?"

His face turned bright red. He opened his mouth to say something, thought better of it, turned on his heel, and strode away.

I watched Adrian disappear into the distance. I was alone and the path back to the dorm looked very long and very dark. There was a soft rustle in the bushes off to my right. For a moment I froze. Then I heard it again. Someone or something was definitely there. I turned and walked swiftly towards the dorm. A branch snapped and I started to run. I didn't stop until I was inside the building and halfway up the stairs leading to my floor. I collapsed onto a step and had to sit there until my heart stopped pounding, and my breathing slowed to normal. I picked myself up and slowly walked the rest of the way to my room.

Chapter 26

We had been assigned a new area to dig. Greg was setting up the screening table. Leslie had gone to the supply tent to get our plastic bags and markers, while Dawna had volunteered to refill our water bottles.

It was hot. I was wiping the sweat from my forehead when Dusty stopped to talk to me. He looked around cautiously then pretended to point out the best place to start digging.

"I'm sorry if I scared you last night, Kate," he said quietly.

"That was you in the bushes?"

"Yes. I went outside to make a phone call. When I heard someone coming I ducked into the shrubbery. You and Adrian started arguing and it was kind of embarrassing to reveal myself so I stayed hidden."

I laughed. "Not totally hidden. I heard you moving around and decided to run for it. I may have over-reacted but someone had searched my room earlier in the week. So I panicked."

His face changed. "What do you mean searched your room?"

I explained about my driver's license being in the wrong place. "And I thought the screws had been loosened on the bolt on my door. I may have been mistaken about that; I never really looked at it before."

Dusty glanced at a point over my head. "Keep up the good work, Kate." And he left.

Sal came up to me. "What did Wendell want?"

"We were talking about where to dig. What do you think—this corner or the other one?"

At dinner that night, I sat with my team. Adrian and Dusty shared a table in the corner. They were deep in conversation. As I was leaving, Dusty motioned me over. "Kate, that little problem you had has been fixed." He glared at Adrian.

Adrian couldn't meet my eyes. With his head down, he muttered, "Sorry, Kate, I shouldn't have left you to walk back to the dorm alone. I let anger get the better of my judgment."

I still didn't understand what I had done to make him angry, but I nodded anyway.

He stood. "I'll walk you back."

"No need; it's still light. I don't need an escort."

He made as if to intercept me but I dodged around him and ducked out the door.

As I walked back to the dorm, Cynthia came up behind me. "Are you adding Wendell to your list of conquests?" she asked, with a sneer on her face.

"Probably not," I replied lightly, "since he will be grading my work, too. We wouldn't want any appearance of impropriety, would we? Though I expect to get the grade I've earned. No more, no less."

She flushed a dull red, turned on her heels and walked away.

When I got back to my room it was to find that the bolt on my door had been replaced with a sturdy, new one.

Chapter 27

The next morning, Sal announced that Wendell was going to show the results of the photography session in the dining hall after dinner.

I couldn't wait to see his presentation. After we finished eating, the screen was set up and Dusty started his slide show. The first photograph showed an aerial view of the entire site. It was amazing—almost like looking at an illustrated map. The paper plates, which showed up as white dots, outlined the whole excavation. Where there were spaces it was easy to see a partial outline and fill in the blanks for ourselves.

Though we had seen no sign of the sun-watch pole, a feature of 12th century Native American sites and which should have been at the center of the settlement, there was a lone paper plate that looked to be in the middle of the marked palisade. Dusty pointed it out as a likely spot. Our 12th century, Late Woodland Indians were no longer just a name in history books. We had dug up the land they occupied and found they were real people with real lives. Their homes, pottery and tools had been under the earth waiting to be found. They caught fish from the river, hunted deer, grew corn, all of which provided sustenance for the village. I didn't want the dig to end. There was so much more to learn.

On Thursday, toward the end of a long week, the van dropped us off early. I walked down the field ahead of my team to the excavation site. A few puffy, white clouds floated across the brilliant blue sky. The sun turned the lazily, flowing waters of White River into a sparkling incandescence. As I got closer I saw a line of dainty, deer tracks circumnavigating the site, before heading in the direction of the river. The previous day we had unearthed butchered deer bone in an ancient midden. Seeing the deer tracks almost took my breath away—the deer had lived here longer than our 12th Century Indians and their descendants were still roaming the same fields.

Leslie broke my reverie. "You want to dig first or screen?" Then she saw the hoof prints. "Oh, how beautiful."

We smiled at each other and shared the moment until Cynthia's sour face reminded us to start the day's work.

I was on my way to dinner, when I heard, "You have a minute, Kate?"

It was Adrian. He gently took my arm and steered me away from the path toward a nearby bench under a shade tree.

"Look, I'm sorry about the other night. I shouldn't have lost my temper. I should have made sure you got back to your room safely."

"I'm sorry I upset you." Though I still didn't understand what I had done.

"Kate, I'm not gay. Why did you think I was?"

"Oh." For a moment I was speechless. "I was told you were..."

"It was Sal, right?"

I reluctantly nodded.

"Look, a few years ago, I was on a dig with a woman who wouldn't take no for an answer. When she realized I truly wasn't interested she started the rumor that I had rejected her because I was gay. I didn't bother to deny it. It was a convenient way to get rid of a person who had become a nuisance." He shrugged. "If I meet someone who—shall we say—interests me, they soon find out the truth. Sal still believes it, though."

"She told me that's why you weren't interested in Cynthia."

He laughed. "No, I'm just not a fan of bitter, angry women."

As we stood to walk to the dining hall, he asked, "Tell me, is the ex still an ex?"

"I don't know. I don't think so."

"In other words, you're not ready to give up on the relationship."

"No, Adrian. I don't think I am."

He strode away, leaving me standing there.

Dawna caught up with me. "Hey, Kate, what did you do to upset Adrian?"

"Earlier, I told him I thought he was gay and he got very angry with me. That's what we were just talking about."

"You told him...?" She started to giggle. The giggles turned into full blown laughter until finally she had to stop and mop her streaming eyes.

"So that's why he asked me out to dinner. Oh, Kate." Her anxious eyes swept over my face. "You don't mind, do you?"

"Mind?" I wasn't sure what she meant for a moment. "You mean about you going to dinner with Adrian? Why would I?"

She gave a sigh of relief. "I've known him for years and I know what he's like. But for someone new..."

"Tell me about him, Dawna. Sal told me he was gay, which is the only reason I went out with him and..."

"He's funny, good company and devilishly handsome, right?"

I shrugged my shoulders. "All true. But he accused me of leading him on."

She started laughing again. "That's rich coming from mister all talk and no action."

"Then he is gay?"

"Nobody really knows. All I can tell you is he dates someone and I know this from personal experience. He's attentive, lots of romantic walks in the moonlight, handholding and goodnight kisses, then nada."

"Nada?"

"He walks the walk, talks the talk and never takes things a step further. The only person with whom he's ever had any kind of lasting relationship is Wendell. They've known each other since college. Wendell is definitely heterosexual so there's nothing there."

"Besides," I asked, "wasn't Wendell married?"

Dawna scowled. "Yes, he was. I don't understand what's wrong with that wife of his. He was so thrilled about the baby then she ups and leaves him and sues for divorce. He used to be such a funny guy always laughing and joking, now he's just plain sad. It's good he has Adrian. For all his faults, he's a loyal friend to Wendell."

Chapter 28

Friday afternoon I was waiting outside the dorm in plenty of time for Sam to pick me up. To my dismay, instead of Sam's black SUV, Frank's old, brown Chevy drew up outside the building and I found he was the one commandeered for chauffeur duty.

I must not have hid my disappointment very well. As he opened the door for me, he said, "Sorry, Kate, something came up at the last minute and Sam couldn't leave."

"What was it?"

Frank looked down at the ground. He didn't seem to know what to say. "Work or something, I think. I'll let him explain it to you."

"But everyone's all right?"

He didn't answer and we drove back to Shelbyville in silence. Something was definitely amiss. I wondered what it was he couldn't tell me but he seemed uncomfortable so I let it go. When we got back to the house, Frank, ever the gentleman, carried my backpack up to the kitchen door.

"I know Doris will have a meal ready; stay and eat with us."

He averted his face, "Can't." Then muttered something about, "things to do," and couldn't get down the stairs fast enough.

That was strange. Frank lived alone and he almost never turned down one of Doris' home cooked meals. I dragged my backpack into the bedroom and had barely started to pull out my dirty laundry when Doris burst into the front hall. She didn't even knock, which was unusual for her.

"Kate, they arrested Stephen."

The only word to describe her was distraught. Her cheeks were flushed, her gray hair stood up in little peaks and she was wringing her hands. I put an arm around her and led her into the living room. "Calm down and tell me what happened. Where was he and how did they find him?"

She sat down on the couch. I took my usual place in the armchair and leaned forward. "Doris, first tell me who arrested him?"

"Sam."

That explained why he wasn't there to pick me up.

"Where did they find him?"

She hesitated then answered, "In my apartment."

"He was here in the house? For how long?"

"Oh, Kate, it was such a mess. He was staying at..." She stopped herself. "He's been somewhere else since the day he left my place. You know, after it happened."

She took a deep breath and I could see her shoulders start to shake. I took her hand and helped her up. "Let's go into the kitchen. We need tea for this."

After we were comfortably ensconced at the kitchen table over a full pot of steaming tea, I got the rest of the story. Sam had arrived at Doris' front door that morning asking about Stephen. Stephen tried to run out the back but Kevin was waiting outside.

"They took him to the police station and I haven't heard anything since." She added, "I told Stephen not to say a word until he talked to a lawyer."

"When did he come back to your apartment?"

"A couple of weeks ago, the night you came to see the play."

"So, where has he been all this time? I know the whole of the Shelbyville police department has been looking for him."

"He was staying with Margaret."

"But Sam has been over there—more than once. How come he wasn't found before this?"

"Margaret lives on the third floor, so when the police rang her buzzer downstairs, Stephen had enough time to slip out her door and over to Pamela Moore's apartment. He stayed there until Margaret told him it was safe to come back."

"But you still haven't told me why he came back to you. Surely Margaret's place was more secure?"

She hesitated, "Pamela Moore didn't want him in her apartment anymore."

"Why?"

Doris poured herself another cup of tea and took a sip before she answered. "She told Stephen that she and Sam were dating and she wanted to be able to invite him up to her apartment."

She laid her hand over mine. "I'm sorry, honey."

"It's all right, Doris. Sam was never going to ask her out. He's been trying to avoid her."

"Oh." She thought for a moment. "But that night when you came to the theater, she told all of us that she wasn't coming to the cast party at Sebastian's place because she was meeting Sam at Luigi's. I believed her."

I nodded. "Sam helped her with a problem she had with her ex-husband and I guess she mistook his kindness for interest. She's been following him all over town. By the time he realized what was happening and put a stop to it she'd convinced herself that he was interested in her."

Doris shook her head in disgust. "Stupid woman. So I've been mad at Sam for nothing. There's another thing, Kate. That other man, the one in the hospital, he's recovering but he doesn't know who attacked him. He says he was sitting in his chair and had his back to whoever it was. All he felt was the knife across his throat." She stopped. "Maybe you shouldn't say anything about that to Sam. I heard from someone at the hospital and I don't know if people are supposed to know yet. The nurse who told me might get into trouble."

"Who was the man? I don't even know his name."

"He was the youth leader at the church that Stephen's uncle attended."

"Where was he found?"

"In the church education room. One of the women who was doing the altar flowers, Edna Sturvey—her sister's in my quilting circle—went in to get some water and that's where he was. His throat was cut and and there was blood everywhere but they got him to the hospital in time. Her sister said Edna screamed and fainted and they had to take her to the hospital too."

I could only imagine.

Chapter 29

The buzzer on my intercom sounded. "It's Detective Kevin Myers, Mrs. Conley."

Doris and I looked at each other. By the formality of the greeting we both knew it was official business.

"I'm going. I'll use the back stairs." She opened the kitchen door and disappeared.

When I got to my front door, Sam stood there alone. "Kevin and I are here to talk to Doris but I wanted to ask you a few questions first."

The last time I saw Sam, he had driven me down to Bloomington. That day we seemed to be resolving our differences and I had wondered if our relationship could be repaired. Today there was an air of reserve about him, a coldness that I found hard to understand.

I led him into the living room and sat in my usual armchair. At first I thought he was going to remain standing, but he eventually sat on the couch opposite.

He watched my face intently. "How long have you known that Stephen Wills was hiding out in Doris' apartment?"

"Since about thirty minutes ago."

His face cleared. "So Doris never told you he was staying with her?"

"No. She just came up to tell me that you'd arrested him."

"He's not under arrest, Kate. We need to question him before he disappears again. And we need to question Doris."

"You said questions, Sam. What other questions do you have for me?"

The antagonism returned. "When were you going to tell me that someone had searched your room? I had to learn that from Dr. Carter."

"I started to call you but it was late, and there wasn't anything you could do. Nothing was stolen."

"Dr. Carter said whoever it was had seen your driver's license. So they now know where you live."

I sighed, "I know."

"And the loose bolt on your door?"

"I thought someone had loosened the screws but if you saw how old the dorms are you'll see that I could easily be mistaken about that."

"But it's fixed now, right? Anything else I should know?"

I reluctantly told him about my conversation with Adrian.

"So he's not gay."

"I guess not."

"And these dinners with him were romantic dates, not two business colleagues meeting after work?"

I squirmed slightly. "I was wrong about that. Someone who should have known told me he was gay and that's why he had no interest in Cynthia."

"But he does have an interest in you?"

"Sam, I don't want to talk about Adrian anymore."

He stood and walked towards the door. "Fair enough." He turned back to me. "Where does that leave us?"

"Is there still an 'us,' Sam?"

"I'm hoping there is but it's your decision. You tell me, Kate." I was so stunned I couldn't answer and after a few seconds of waiting Sam left.

Chapter 30

I was sitting in the bar at Luigi's in front of a small salad that I didn't want and a large glass of wine that I did. It started with Doris and her cooking. She loved to cook and feed people anyway, but when she was upset it was a compulsion she couldn't control. The aromas of lasagna, fried chicken, macaroni and cheese coupled with pineapple upside-down cake and blueberry pie permeated the whole house. I was invited to dinner but when I got downstairs I found all our friends were there too, and the only topic of conversation seemed to be Sam and how badly he had treated Stephen.

Sebastian was furious. "How could Sam arrest Stephen?"

I tried to reason with him, "He's not arrested. He's been taken in for questioning."

"But Sam knows he couldn't have anything to do with something so brutal."

"He was there, at the barn, the night of the murder. Sam has to interview him."

There was silence. All conversation ceased and the atmosphere became very constrained. Since I had defended Sam, nobody wanted to say anything about Stephen while I was there. Finally, I could take it no longer. I left, pleading a headache and an early night.

I was still hungry so when I got back to my apartment I called a cab, told the driver to wait for me in the alley, crept down the backstairs, and had him drop me off at Luigi's. When Sam left the precinct that was where he would most likely go to eat. The restaurant was crowded and the only available table was in the bar.

I was hoping to keep a low profile but Pamela Moore came in and ruined that. She saw me and immediately came over to the table. I ignored her until she finally said, "Hi, Kate; all alone this evening?"

"For now," I answered.

"Are you waiting for Sam?"

I didn't say anything, just sipped my wine.

"He's tied up at the station."

"I know."

"I'm waiting for him too." This said defiantly.

"Well, don't let me keep you." I finished my wine and gestured to the server for another.

Pamela wandered over to the bar and sat on one of the stools. She started a conversation with someone sitting around the corner out of my line of sight.

Coming to the restaurant had been a mistake. The fact that she was waiting for Sam depressed me. I believed him when he said he had never dated her and she'd fantasized a relationship with him. Yet, I had trusted my ex-husband implicitly, until I caught him having sex with his new secretary two days after we celebrated our 30th wedding anniversary. *Sam was nothing like Jack*, I told myself but the thought persisted.

I checked the time. It was getting late and Sam was very likely still at the station questioning Stephen. I decided to go home, and called for my tab. As I waited for the server to bring back my card, I saw someone grab Pamela Moore by the arm. She pulled away, terrified. I heard a screamed, "No, no! That's not true. You're lying!" Whoever it was had their back to me, people were crowding around them and I couldn't see who it was.

Pamela leaned forward and tried to say something. She was pushed away and almost fell off the stool. I saw the bartender leap over the counter and grab the person. He pulled her into my line of sight. It was Sal.

He said something to her in a low tone. She knocked his arms down. "Don't worry; I'm going, I'm going."

Sal staggered away from him and made her way to my table. As the waiter stood there open-mouthed, she screamed at me. "You lied! You were lying all the time!" Her voice rose to a crescendo, "You pretended to be my friend and all the time you were plotting to get Dusty away from me!"

Patrons stood back as she stormed out of the bar. She pushed the front door back on its hinges so violently it crashed against the wall. Pamela Moore hurried past me.

I grabbed her. "What did you say to make her so angry?"

"Nothing."

She tried to pull away but I held onto her.

"Tell me."

"She asked me if you were still dating Sam. She called him your boyfriend."

"What did you say?"

She gave me a defiant look. "I told her no, that Sam and I are dating. That I was waiting in the bar for him."

"What else?"

"Just what everyone is saying, that you and Dusty Carter are getting married. And..."

I opened my mouth and she quickly said, "Barbara Armstrong told me. She said everyone knows it."

"Anything else?"

She looked defiant. "And you flirt with every man you see."

She saw the anger on my face and flinched. "Well, you were having dinner with another man last week and you still are hanging onto Sam."

"Pamela," I said through gritted teeth, "I know that you and Sam aren't dating. That's a little fantasy you've concocted. Sam and I are still together."

Her eyes filled with tears. "I don't believe you. You broke up."

"And now we've reconciled." I wasn't sure that was entirely true but I was determined to find out one way or the other.

I grabbed my card and receipt, asked Luigi to call a cab for me, and left her standing at my table.

There were no cars parked in front of the house but Doris' lights were on. That meant her apartment door was probably still standing open. I was in no mood to face her. I asked the cab driver to drop me in the alley. That way I could sneak up the back stairs without being seen.

I crossed the yard and paused to dig into my purse for my house keys, which is why I didn't notice Sal until she was right in front of me.

She grabbed me by the arm. "When were you going to tell me about you and Dusty?"

Her eyes glittered in the residual light from the security pole in the alley.

Her intensity made me nervous. "There's nothing to tell, Sal. Dusty and I went to high school together but lost touch when he went to college."

Her grip tightened. "And now you're both divorced you think you can come back into his life and take up where you left off all those years ago?"

"You're wrong, Sal. I'm dating someone else."

She was beginning to scare me. Her face was shiny with sweat and her mouth was twitching. "You and the policeman broke up. He's dating Pamela Moore now. You dumped him as soon as Dusty came back in town."

I tried to edge around her toward the back door but she blocked me. She was holding something down at her side. "You're not going to do to Dusty what you've done to the other men in your life. You got rid of your husband and your lover when you heard he was coming back to Indiana."

"Sal, you're mistaken. I divorced Jack over a year ago. I had no idea Dusty would be in charge of the dig. I hadn't seen him in thirty years." I tried to speak in a calm soothing tone but it seemed to enrage her more.

"You prey on any man you can find. Pamela told me." She lifted her arm and I saw the machete she was concealing. "All these years I've protected Dusty from women like you. I take care of him. He needs me." I backed away from her. The rage was building as fast as an out of control forest fire.

I was almost to the back porch when she yelled, "Stop!"

I froze. The strangled scream that came from her distorted mouth sounded like the howl of a wild animal. She rushed toward me. I turned and tried to run but I wasn't fast enough. She raised the machete over her head. It had started on its downward arc when a body hurtled through the air. I was violently pushed to one side while an arm came out and punched Sal in the face. Her head snapped back and she went down. As she fell the machete slashed and made contact.

I dropped and hit my head on the back step. My knee connected with something sharp. Someone fell beside me. It was Sam. Blood gushed out of his neck and shoulder. Panic stricken, I tore off my scarf wadded it up and pressed it against the wound but it wasn't stemming the flow.

Sam groaned, "Kate." He was looking past me and trying to get up.

Sal had struggled to her feet. She still had the now bloody, machete in her hand. She straightened, staggered slightly and moved toward me. Sam made one more effort to push himself up and fell back unconscious.

There was a slight whooshing noise, something rushed past my head. It glistened in the dim light. Sal staggered for a moment, moaned, then slowly keeled over and lay twitching on the grass.

I looked up. Doris was standing on the back porch. The black object she had been holding in her hand fell to the ground.

Her voice quavered, "She's not dead, is she?"

The house door opened with a crash. Rose and Enid rushed out. Enid caught Doris as she crumpled to the ground. Rose ran to Sal and stood over her, a large iron skillet in her hand.

I heard sirens, pounding feet then a couple of EMT's set me to one side and started working on Sam. Two officers grabbed Sal and cuffed her hands behind her. I heard one of them ask, "Whose taser is this?"

Sam was hustled into an ambulance and rushed away. I was strapped to a stretcher and placed in another. Doris came with me and we held onto each other all the way to the hospital.

Chapter 31

The first person I saw as the EMT's were wheeling my gurney into the ER was Martha. She was standing in a group of law enforcement officers with her back to me. It looked as if the whole of the Shelbyville police department was at the hospital. I tried to sit up to attract her attention but the EMT's had me strapped down and we were moving rapidly along a long corridor towards one of the triage rooms.

"How's Sam?" I managed to call back to her.

I didn't get an answer but heard Doris ask the same question as she was taken in a different direction.

Kevin stood to one side of the corridor. As my gurney was wheeled past, I called out to him. He hurried over and I was finally able to get an answer to my question.

"He's in surgery, Kate."

He saw my face and quickly added, "It's nothing life-threatening—just some repair work on his shoulder. I'll give you an update when I..."

His face registered shock as he noticed, for the first time, my torn and bloodstained dress. He quickly stepped back and waved the EMT's on before I could tell him that the blood was Sam's not mine and the EMT's were the ones who had cut my dress to pieces.

After all the blood was cleaned off, the doctor determined all I needed were stitches to a cut on my knee and the scrape on my face cleaned and bandaged. The most severe injury was a slight concussion but since I had been attacked by a machete-wielding maniac I had come out of the encounter pretty well unscathed.

Two detectives whom I'd seen around the station but hadn't met before, came in to question me. They introduced themselves and I promptly forgot their names.

"How's Sam?"

They looked at each other. 'He's not out of surgery yet."

"He's going to be all right?"

"That's what the doctors are telling us, ma'am. Now if you could just recount for us exactly what happened this evening."

I started with why I'd gone to Luigi's in the first place, though I didn't say I was hoping to run into Sam there.

"When you went in did you see the woman who attacked you and Detective Williamson?"

"No. I was sitting by myself in a corner of the bar because the dining room was full. The only person I recognized was an acquaintance of mine, Pamela Moore."

"Did you speak to her?"

"She came over and spoke to me."

"What did she say?"

I tried to recall the conversation. "She asked if I was waiting for Sam and told me he was at the precinct. Which I knew," I added. I massaged my aching head then wished I hadn't when my fingers encountered the painful lump I'd received. "Sam and Kevin had taken Stephen Wills in for questioning."

"When did you first see Sal Granger?"

"I saw Pamela Moore talking to someone who was sitting around the corner of the bar. I couldn't see who that someone was. There were raised voices and she was standing in front of Pamela. She pushed her back on the stool and turned around. That's when I saw it was Sal. She came toward me..."

I had to stop and take a few deep breaths. "She came toward me and screamed at me then left by the front door, slamming it behind her."

"What exactly did she say?"

"That I'd lied to her about not knowing Dusty."

"That's Doctor Carter."

"Right—he was being..."

"We know about the stalking. You knew Dr. Carter prior to working on the dig with him?"

"Yes, we dated during high school and broke off the relationship when he started college. I hadn't seen him in thirty years."

"Did you know he was married?"

"I did. Dusty told me about the stalker and we decided it was safer not to tell anyone we knew each other previously."

The questions went on and by the time we got to what Pamela Moore had said to Sal, which tipped her over the edge, I was so exhausted I could scarcely frame a coherent answer.

The nurse came into the room and told them they had to leave.

The heavyset officer said, "Just one more question. You knew the woman who slashed Detective Williamson's shoulder, is that correct?"

"Yes, we were working together on an archeological dig in southern Indiana. I thought she was a friend. I had no idea..." I couldn't go on. I buried my head in my hands, my breath coming in shuddering sobs.

The nurse opened the door. "Out, now."

The two police officers left.

She came over, handed me a glass of sweet orange juice, waited until I drank it, then tucked a warm blanket around me and told me to rest.

"Are you awake, Kate?"

I opened my eyes to see Sam's daughter, Mira, bending over me. I struggled up on one elbow. "How long have I been asleep?"

"A couple of hours. Dad's out of surgery and in recovery. He wants to see you."

"Is he all right, Mira?"

Mira sat on the edge of the bed. "Yes, it was basically repair work. It's going to take a few weeks for the shoulder to heal and he won't be back on active duty without a course of physical therapy, but he should make a complete recovery."

I sat up and looked around, then realized I had no clothes except the skimpy hospital gown I was wearing. Mira handed me a set of scrubs. "The nurse left these for you. What you were wearing is toast. The EMT's literally cut them off you."

With Mira's help, I quickly dressed. I couldn't find my shoes so I went barefoot. Two nurses stared at me as we walked down the corridor but nobody stopped me and we reached the elevator unchallenged.

When we emerged, Doris was sitting in the waiting room. Before I could ask if she were all right, she announced, "They took him to his room already. It's this way."

She trotted down the hallway ahead of us and stopped outside a room that had a police officer standing outside. He evidently recognized Mira because he opened the door and let us in.

I followed her into the room. Sam was propped up in the bed with his left shoulder heavily bandaged and his arm resting on a pile of pillows. His eyes were closed, his face pale and he looked completely exhausted.

I went over to him and gently stroked his face. He opened his eyes and held out his undamaged arm to me.

"Kate. Are you hurt?"

I collapsed onto the bed next to him. "No."

The tears started and I buried my face in his undamaged shoulder. He held me close and we stayed like that until a nurse came into the room and told me I had to leave.

Chapter 32

"Sam, how did you know about Sal? Why were you in the yard when she attacked me?"

After a few hours sleep, I drove to the hospital to spend some time alone with Sam. He looked a lot better than he had earlier that morning.

I was sitting on his bed. Sam had his arm around me holding me close. His injured shoulder was propped up with pillows and everything felt absolutely right with us.

"Ever since your tires were slashed at Luigi's, I've asked the staff to watch for any strange incidents. When that woman created a scene, the bartender called me and filled me in on the conversation between her and Pamela Moore and the fact that she had left in such a violent rage. When I found out you left shortly after her, I went straight to your house, and thank god I did."

He lightly touched the side of my face that was bandaged. "You're sure you're all right?"

"Sam, it was just a couple of scrapes and a bump on the head. I'm fine."

"And Doris? She really put that crazy woman down with a taser?"

"Yes, she probably saved both our lives."

I shuddered, reliving the moment when Sal had staggered to her feet and come toward us, the machete raised over her head, screaming like a banshee. The prongs of the taser had hit her squarely in the chest and dropped her like a stone. I still had a hard time believing that friendly, jolly Sal was Dusty's stalker and she was so delusional she was prepared to kill to keep a man who regarded her as nothing more than a colleague.

Sam dropped a kiss on the top of my head. "It'll get better, Kate."

I relaxed into him. He felt warm and safe.

The door opened. Mira put her head around it and peered into the room.

"Can we talk to you, Dad?"

The 'we' included Doris who followed her in.

"I have to go back to Cincinnati tomorrow and Kate has to get to Bloomington. You'll need someone to take care of you when you're released from the hospital."

Sam looked bewildered. "I can go back to my apartment. I'll be fine by myself."

"No, you won't," said Doris firmly. "I'm going to take care of you. You can stay with me. I have a spare bedroom."

I saw the look of panic flash across Sam's face and quickly interjected, "Actually, I was thinking of skipping the last week of the dig. I can take care of Sam."

He shook his head. "No way Kate; I'm not letting you give that up for me. I can stay in my own place."

"With one functioning arm? How do you think you can manage that?" Mira's voice rose. "No, Dad. Besides you'll never get any rest there. People will be stopping by to see you constantly. You'll stay with Doris and she can look after you."

I broke in hurriedly, "What if your father stays in my apartment? Nobody will be there so he'll have the privacy he needs and Doris can still take care of him."

"Works for me, "Doris said. "It would be quiet for Sam and I'm downstairs when he needs something."

That seemed an acceptable solution to all concerned and we stayed until Sam leaned back on his pillows, closed his eyes and the nurse told us leave.

Chapter 33

Gloom hung over the dig site like a dark thundercloud. Dusty hadn't told the students the reason for Sal's absence but his dour face contributed to the grim atmosphere. I attributed my various cuts and bruises to a fallacious, fall downstairs, but Dusty and I realized that as soon as the news media picked up the story everyone would know. He was hoping it wouldn't happen before the end of the week.

"I still can't believe it, Kate." We were sitting in a patch of shade at the edge of the field. Students walked up to us then quickly turned away after seeing the less than welcoming look Dusty gave them. Even Adrian and Cynthia decided against joining us. "I've known Sal since my first dig in Belize. She was the one who suggested I use my middle name. She said I wouldn't be taken seriously in academia with a name like Dusty. I loved having her on my digs because she was so efficient and good with the students and all the time…" he took a breath, "she was the one threatening my family. She killed my dog. Hell, Kate, she would have killed you and Detective Williamson. How could I not have seen what she was?"

"Don't beat yourself up, Dusty; I liked her, too. She was the last person I would have thought of as being dangerous. She was always so helpful and friendly." Except for the last time when I saw her rushing towards Sam and me, with a machete held high in her hand. I shuddered when I thought of how close Sam had come to dying.

Dusty squeezed my hand. "At least the nightmare is finally over. I can go back to my life and Sheila, Lily and I can live like a normal family again."

It was over except for the bad dreams which I'd had for the past two nights. I wondered if Sam had bad dreams too or if his training and experience had somehow inured him. More than anything I wanted to finish up the dig and get back home to him.

In the distance I saw Adrian lift his arm and tap his watch. Our signal that lunch was over. Cynthia was waiting at our site. She opened her mouth to say something. I looked at her and waited. I don't know what she saw on my face but she backed away and left to harass another group of students.

Lesley looked up. "I'm glad she's gone. There's something really nasty about that woman."

"She's mad at me," Dawna replied, "I went to lunch with Adrian yesterday and she's done nothing but snarl at me ever since."

"At least she's an equal opportunity hater," I said.

Lesley giggled. "I'm going to dinner with Adrian tonight so add me to the list."

"How about you, Greg? Do you want to be on the list too?" But Greg had unearthed another pottery fragment and was oblivious to our banter.

I had hated leaving Shelbyville with Stephen still at police headquarters and Sam hospitalized with a slashed shoulder. Doris called to tell me Sam was out of the hospital and safely settled in my apartment. She was making sure that only Kevin and Mira knew where he was. Stephen had been released and was staying with Sebastian. The few times I was able to call Sam, I had awakened him from a deep sleep, so I limited my calls to texts, telling myself I would see him in a few days and we could catch up then.

I was intensely angry with Pamela Moore and Bitch Barbara for spreading the gossip which had resulted in Sam's injury. Doris told me that Pamela Moore had turned up at the house bearing a basket of fruit for Sam, wanting to know where he was.

"No way was I going to tell her. I sent her away with a flea in her ear and threw her fruit basket after her. She was responsible for almost getting both of you killed, and I told her it would be a cold day in hell before she got any information out of me."

I knew I could trust Doris as gate-keeper.

I was sitting cross-legged in the bottom of the pit working on another organic stain. Kneeling on my stitched knee was painful so I was trying to keep weight off it. A shadow loomed over me. It was Cynthia. I knew by the sneer on her face that she was going to say something unpleasant.

"I see Adrian has dumped you for someone else."

I smiled. "Yes, he has. Actually it's two 'some-ones.' He's dating Lesley as well as Dawna."

"Is that why you're trying to get your hooks into Wendell now?"

"You know, you're really stupid. Wendell is married and has a child. What we talk about has nothing to do with you."

She stood there for a moment. Then, finding no suitable rejoinder, walked away. I ignored her for the rest of the week. I did worry about my grade but at our final meeting before everyone left, Dusty announced we had all passed the course and grades would be sent out the following week.

Chapter 34

It felt good to be finally home. Digger greeted me with his usual enthusiastic licks and followed me throughout the apartment as I unpacked my suitcase and backpack. There was no sign of Sam and no trace of his belongings. There was no trace of Doris either.

After waiting an hour, I called Kevin.

"He's down here at the precinct, Kate. They're questioning Pamela Moore again about the night of the attack."

Just then Doris came in carrying bags of groceries. She looked upset. "I'm glad you're home, Kate. You've got to talk to Sam. He went back to his own place yesterday but he's not well enough to take care of himself."

I put my arm around her shoulder. "Don't worry, Doris. I just talked to Kevin. Sam's at the precinct. I'm going there right now and I'll make sure he comes back here with me."

When I got through the various layers of security, I finally tracked Sam down in the corridor outside the interrogation rooms. He looked up, smiled, and moved toward me. One of the doors opened and the two detectives who had questioned me at the hospital came out. Pamela Moore followed them. Her face lit up when she saw Sam but I got there first. He enfolded me in a crushing embrace. I lifted my face to his and when we came up for air, Pamela had disappeared.

I steered Sam into an empty side room. "Why did you leave my apartment?"

The tips of his ears turned red, a sure sign he was embarrassed. "It was just until today. I was coming back as soon as you got home."

"But why leave?"

"I...oh hell, Kate, I couldn't stay any longer."

"Why not?"

He dropped his head. "Doris has been great. I mean she's fed me and kept visitors away but..."

"But?"

"Kate, she wanted to give me a bath."

I tried not to laugh. "A bath?"

"Trying to take a shower one-handed isn't easy. I covered my dressing with a plastic bag but it got wet anyway. Enid and Doris had to take me back to the doctor to have a new dressing applied. He suggested I should take baths instead of showers. That's when Doris said she would help me. I wasn't sure how far the help would go so I had Kevin take me to my apartment last night."

I slid my arms around his waist. "If I promise to protect you from Doris will you come back?"

He grinned at me. "Absolutely."

As I led him to the door, he said, "Though, Kate, I wouldn't object if you wanted to..."

"Don't push your luck, Sam."

Chapter 35

"Are you glad to be going back to work?"

Sam poured himself a cup of coffee and sat down opposite me at the kitchen table before he answered. "Yes and no. I will hate being confined to desk duty. But until the physical therapy is over that's how it has to be. It will give me time to catch up on paper work." He smiled at me across the table. "The last two weeks here with you have been..." he flushed slightly and cleared his throat. "You know, Kate."

"I do. And now you have to go back to your own apartment?" It was a question rather than a statement.

"Yes, because I don't think you're ready to make this a permanent arrangement. Or are you?" This said hopefully.

"Not quite yet, Sam."

"Guess I'll have to be satisfied with that for now."

He took a last swig of coffee, kissed me on top of the head and dashed for the back door. I heard his footsteps clattering down the stairs.

I stirred my tea thoughtfully. I would miss Sam but I wasn't ready to have us move in together. For one thing, Sam was a very private person. I was sure he wouldn't be happy staying in the same house with four women. Sharing his apartment wasn't an option. I loved living with Doris, Enid and Rose, too much. But most of all, my apartment was the first time I had anything that was just mine. I had chosen every piece of furniture, decorated each room and, though I had no problem with Sam leaving a few clothes in my closet, I didn't want to re-arrange my whole life to make room for him—not yet anyway.

There was an insistent knock on my front door. I waited a few seconds then went to answer it.

"Is Sam gone?" Doris asked.

"Yes."

"Is he moving back into his own place?"

She followed me into the kitchen. I poured a cup of coffee and put it in front of her.

"Yes, neither of us is ready to make this permanent."

Doris gave an emphatic snort.

"What's that supposed to mean?"

"It's you who doesn't want to make this permanent." She pursed her lips. "Don't keep him waiting too long, that's all I'm saying. Has Pamela Moore stopped calling you?"

"Yes. I told her I didn't want to talk to her. I'm not ready to accept any apologies."

"I should think not. The stupid woman almost got you and Sam killed with her lies."

I took a deep breath. "If it hadn't been for you and your taser I don't know what would have happened."

"Lucky I bought that, huh?"

Given her track record with guns, I couldn't believe Doris had hit her target the first time she used her new toy. But I was thankful she had. I still had nightmares of Sam lying on the ground bleeding in my arms, while a madwoman struggled to her feet and came towards us brandishing a blood-stained machete. The scenario played over and over in my head in an endless loop, waking me up at night. Until today, Sam had been there when the bad dreams came, but from now on I would be on my own.

Doris topped up her coffee. "You never told me what Sam said about the interrogation."

"Because he was personally involved, he couldn't sit in on it. But Kevin was there. He said Barbara Armstrong told Pamela I was planning on marrying Dusty. She also told her that I had dumped my ex-husband and Sam for him. That's why Pamela thought she had a shot with Sam."

"But he couldn't stand her, surely she could see that."

"I think people make their own reality, Doris. Because she wanted it to be true she believed it."

"Do you think she's given up on him?"

"I hope so, but I don't know."

Doris thought about that for a moment. "What about that Adrian? Are you going to see him again?"

"No. He was only a friend. Now he knows I'm not interested, he's on to someone else." I filled her in on Dawna and Leslie's theory."

Doris gave another of her snorts. "So what you're saying is, he's all talk and no trousers."

When I was able to stop laughing, I answered her. "That pretty much sums it up, Doris."

Chapter 36

Sylvia was sitting at the librarian's desk working at her computer. I wheeled my cart of books over to her. "What's with Sebastian today?"

"You mean why is he walking around with that stupid grin on his face?" Sylvia replied.

"Yes, ever since the body in the barn was discovered he's been a snarling tiger. Now he looks as if he's won the lottery."

"I think Kate it's something to do with Stephen."

I laughed. "It usually is."

"Check with Doris; she'll know."

Actually, Doris had wanted to tell me something that morning I was late for my library shift and told her we'd talk later. Sure enough, the minute I set foot in my back door, Doris was knocking at the front.

"Did you hear about Sebastian and Stephen?"

She followed me throughout the apartment as I changed out of my work clothes into something more comfortable.

"I know that Sebastian was going around grinning like the Cheshire cat today."

Doris was grinning too. "Stephen has moved in with Sebastian and he's thinking of opening his own shop in Shelbyville to save the long commute. He's no longer a suspect in either killing."

I hung up my slacks and slipped into a pair of sweats. "Sam says Stephen was never a viable suspect. There was no physical evidence in the barn and not a trace of blood on his clothes or in his car. The murderer would have been soaked in blood. They needed to question him simply because he was there that night. If he'd called the police right away he would saved himself and everyone else a lot of heartache."

Doris had the grace to look ashamed. She dropped her head and muttered something about "thought it was for the best," then, "guess I should apologize to Sam for not trusting him."

"We're meeting at Luigi's tonight for dinner. Come with us and you can apologize then."

Doris and I were sitting in Luigi's, sipping our wine and waiting for Sam. He was coming straight from work and meeting us there. The restaurant was busy and I had trouble finding a parking space and finally ended up in the back lot.

Doris had gone to a lot of trouble getting dressed for tonight. She wore her 'best' outfit and had had her hair in pink, plastic curlers all day. The end result wasn't all that different from the way her hair usually looked but it seemed important to Doris so Enid, Rose and I had commented on how stylish it looked. She would occasionally reach up and pat the tight little curls.

"Hello, Kate, Doris." Pamela Moore was standing next to our table, a hopeful look plastered on her face. She was like one of those annoying little flies that keep buzzing around no matter how much you swat them. I had successfully avoided her until now but evidently she hadn't given up trying.

"What do you want, Pamela?" My tone wasn't exactly welcoming but that didn't seem to deter her. She tried to pull out the chair next to me but I hooked my foot around the cross-bar and held on. She struggled for a moment then gave up.

"I wanted to apologize for telling that woman about you and Dusty Carter. I thought it was true. If I'd had any idea what she was going to do…"

"Really, you thought it was true? Do you pass on every piece of salacious gossip you're told? Or was it because you wanted it to be true?"

"Well, you had broken up with Sam. I thought..."

"That you'd be there to pick up the pieces."

Her eyes filled with tears. I flashed back to the red, raw scar on Sam's neck and shoulder. I had no sympathy for her. I could barely stand speaking to the woman, let alone accept an apology from her.

Doris stood up. "You'd best go. We don't want you anywhere around us."

Pamela opened her mouth to plead, thought better of it and rushed toward the front door.

Sam entered almost simultaneously through the side entrance from the parking lot. "Is there any wine left in that bottle or are you two going to drink it all?"

Doris quickly poured him a glass. He raised it to us, "To dinner with two, beautiful women."

Doris smiled and patted her hair again.

At least Bitch Barbara and her groupies waited until we finished dessert. I would have hated having my tiramisu ruined by her particular brand of venom.

"Kate, what a surprise. You're dining with Detective Williamson. Wasn't your handsome, new boyfriend available or has he found someone else already?" The little coterie of hags standing behind her, giggled into their hands.

Sam smiled up at her. It wasn't a pleasant smile. "It's been really bugging me but now I've remembered who you are—Nellie Wiedermeyer. You were three years ahead of me in high school."

Barbara gave an uncertain smile. "You've got me confused with someone else. I'm Barbara Armstrong."

"You are now, but you were Nellie when I knew you. You and your family lived in that old rental out on the Peterson farm. Your father worked for him until your brother blew up the house cooking meth."

I heard a few indrawn breaths as a wave of interest went around the women crowded by the table. The focus of attention shifted from me to Barbara.

Sam smiled again. "How is Jason? He should be up for parole soon."

Her face turned scarlet. "You bastard," she hissed. She pushed past her entourage and headed towards the front door, the women scurrying behind her like a gaggle of geese.

Sam laughed. "I know that was a mean and despicable thing to do, but damn, it felt good. Maybe now she'll leave us alone."

Doris piped up, "You know her husband's divorcing her, don't you? He dated Janeen Kelly in high school but a rumor went around that she was pregnant and they split up. By the time Robert found out it wasn't true, she'd met someone else. Everyone says he married that Barbara woman on the rebound. Janeen Kelly is widowed now and it looks as if the relationship is on again."

I was awestruck. "Doris, you never lived in Shelbyville until a year ago. How do you know all this?"

She shrugged her shoulders. "I hear things. They say Barbara Armstrong's taken to drink."

"Well, she's always here hanging out at the bar."

"Wonder who started the pregnancy rumor?" said Sam.

Doris and I looked at each other. We both snorted into our glass of wine. When we left it was to find all four tires on my car had been slashed again.

Chapter 37

Ex-husbands never go away, especially if there are children involved. A couple of days after my tires were slashed for the second time, I got a phone call from Jack.

"What do you want?" I snapped. It was early and he should have known better than to expect civility before I was fully awake.

He said hurriedly, "We need to talk to Ellie. I'm afraid she's going to destroy her marriage with this crazy idea she has of going back to school."

"Explain to me how going back to school will destroy her marriage."

"She has a husband and children to take care of."

"The husband is old enough to take care of himself. She can arrange childcare for the twins. There's no reason she can't take classes."

"But she doesn't need to do it. She's got this idea of getting a job. Andrew is well able to support his family. His mother was perfectly happy taking care of him and his father."

"His mother is the most stupid woman I know and his father is a serial philanderer. They're hardly the role models I want for our daughter. And Ellie doesn't want a job, Jack. She wants a career. That way, if her husband decides to cheat on her, she would be able to support herself and the children."

There was silence, then the sound of the phone disconnecting.

A few minutes later, it rang again. I picked it up. "What now?"

It was Sam. "Wow. Should I call back later?"

"Sorry, no. I thought you were my stupid ex-husband."

"Do you want to have some tea or something then call me back once you've calmed down?"

"I'm okay now, Sam. Why are you calling?"

"The night we had dinner at Luigi's with Doris, did you upset anyone other than Barbara Armstrong?"

"You were the one who upset Barbara Armstrong, not me. But Doris and I did have a few words with Pamela Moore."

"About what?"

"She keeps trying to apologize for what she said to Sal Granger but I don't feel like absolving her of guilt just so she can feel better."

"Okay, so those two?"

"Do you think one of them slashed my tires?"

"Could be; they were at the restaurant both times."

"But which one?"

"That's what we have to figure out."

"I think we should throw a party."

"I'm all for that, Doris, but what are we celebrating?"

She thought for a moment. "Well, Sebastian and Stephen have moved in together, so how about a pre-engagement party?"

"They're going to get engaged?"

Doris shrugged her shoulders. "They haven't said so yet but it's only a matter of time."

I took her word for it. She was usually right. Besides, Sam was working a lot of hours on what Doris and I called the 'barn murders,' even though the second one had taken place in a church and turned out to be an attack not a murder, so my social life was somewhat curtailed. A party sounded like something we all needed.

It had been so long since I'd done any kind of entertaining that I'd forgotten what it entailed. First there was the guest list, library friends, theater friends, family, senior center, quilting circle—it seemed endless.

"Doris, we're not going to have enough space." At last count there were almost fifty people.

"I talked to Enid and Rose. We can use all three apartments for seating and have buffet tables set up in the hallway and landings. We'll use my apartment for the bar. It will all work out."

If only I could be that sanguine!

Then there was the food. That was definitely Doris' department. All she needed from me was freezer, refrigerator and oven use. Rose and Enid were designing and sending out the invitations. Frank and Margaret would help with set-up and serving.

Throwing a 'Doris" party' involved a lot of cooking which meant a lot of shopping. Every day Doris thought of another dish she should prepare which meant another trip to the grocery store. It was on the way back from one of these trips that Doris decided we needed to stop at the butcher's shop.

"I want to make sure my hams will be ready to pick up first thing Saturday morning and the butcher he said he'll try to have some shrimp and scallops for me, too."

The shop was empty when we walked in. We stood there for a few moments clearing throats and shuffling feet. I was about to ring the bell on the counter when we heard raised voices from the back room.

"Shut up, I don't want to hear anything else about it."

Someone answered but it was too low to make out the words. The first voice yelled, "No, I won't listen to you anymore." There was the sound of a scuffle and a muffled exclamation of pain. The butcher came striding out, almost knocking me over. He left through the shop door.

I grasped Doris' arm to stop her from rushing into the back room and called out tentatively, "Are you all right? Do you need help?"

The butcher's wife, Ada, hurried out. "I'm fine. Can I get something for you?"

Doris answered, "I just came by to make sure the things I ordered will be ready to pick up early on Saturday."

She leaned across the counter, "Honey, are you sure we can't help you?"

The woman refused to look at us. "I don't need your help and the order will be ready first thing Saturday."

She walked back into her workroom.

Chapter 38

"You think we should have said something to Sam?"

Doris looked at me anxiously through the thick lenses of her glasses.

"I already did. He's going to have Martha stop in at the shop from time to time to check things out."

Doris had been cooking all day. She slid more desserts into my freezer. It was almost full, as was the refrigerator. "Do you have much more to prepare? We're running out of room."

"No, that's about it. I'm picking up the ham and seafood in the morning. After that it's just last minute stuff."

"How many people are coming?"

Doris did some complicated calculations on her fingers. "About thirty I think—oh no, I forgot the senior center—they're all coming, maybe closer to fifty, or sixty. I'm doing a buffet because not everyone can get here at the same time."

She took a crumpled list from her pocket. "We're going to need more chairs. Frank will bring some. Enid and Rose said a friend of theirs will loan his. We'll put the extra leaves in the dining tables..." She walked around mumbling to herself, checking off items.

I took the list from her hand. "Doris, you've done enough for today. Let's have an early night. Tomorrow's going to be busy."

At some time in the night, I awoke in a cold sweat. My body shook and my heart was racing so fast I could scarcely breathe. The dream was the same as all the others—the machete, Sam lying on the ground with blood pumping from his shoulder and, no matter how much pressure I kept on the wound, the dark pool around him getting larger and larger until the whole yard was awash with his blood. In the background, Sal screaming, and the machete coming down towards us.

I staggered towards the bathroom before I realized there was no blood on me to wash off. The light shocked me fully awake. I couldn't go back to bed. Trying to watch television made things worse. The only program I could find was an old black and white horror movie. It was too close to the nightmare I had just experienced except the movie blood was black not scarlet. Finally, I switched off the set and lay on the couch in the living room. I pulled the throw over me and drifted in and out of an uneasy sleep.

Chapter 39

"Kate, wake up."

I raised myself up on my elbow. "What…?"

I swear I had just fallen asleep and here was Doris shaking me awake already.

"I wanted to tell you I'm going over to the butcher's shop to pick up my order. I should be back in half an hour."

I muttered something, rolled over into my blanket and fell back to sleep. The next thing I heard was the phone. I reached for it then realized it wasn't there. I was on the couch instead of in my bed. The ringing stopped. Someone hammered at my door.

"Kate, it's only us. We've got the chairs Doris wanted."

I staggered to the door to let in Rose and Enid. Rose asked, "Where's Doris? Frank is downstairs and he needs to get into her apartment and drop off his chairs."

I rubbed my eyes. "What time is it?"

"It's almost noon."

"Noon?"

Doris should have been back by now. Last night she'd told me she was going to pick up the hams, first thing. For Doris that meant the minute the shop opened which would have been at nine. As far as I knew that was the only errand she had to run. I woke up fast.

"Here's the spare key to Doris' place. I'm going to drive over to the butcher's shop to see where she is. She might need help carrying her stuff home."

I threw on old sweats, tied back my hair and drove the two blocks to the shop. There was probably a logical explanation for Doris taking so long. I had no idea when she left. I was too sleepy to notice the time.

But, no matter how many times I told myself this, the sick feeling in the pit of my stomach wouldn't go away. Parking was tight and I had to leave the car a block away. I walked into an empty shop and rang the bell on the counter.

"Can I help you?" Ada came in from the back room.

"Yes, has Mrs. Weppler been in to pick up her order yet?"

She looked around and pointed to a large paper-wrapped package sitting in the cold case. "No. Not yet."

"She was supposed to pick it up first thing."

"That's what she told me. It's been ready since we opened."

I tried once more. "And you haven't heard from her—she hasn't called or anything?"

She was getting impatient with my questions. "I haven't seen or heard from her. Now I have to get back…"

I moved towards the door then stopped. Since I was at the shop, I might as well pick up Doris' order for her. Ada had already returned to the back room.

I walked behind the counter and put my head around the door. "Can I take Mrs…?" I broke off as I saw something on the floor by the side of the walk-in freezer. It was Doris' old cream colored purse.

For a moment I stood there stunned, trying to work through the implication of Doris' purse being in the back room of the butcher's shop when the butcher's wife had just told me she hadn't been there this morning. Ada was standing next to her work-table staring at me with a strange expression on her face. In her hand she held a large, very sharp-looking knife.

I tried to act as if I hadn't noticed the purse. "Thanks anyway, she's probably at home by now."

I started to leave but she moved swiftly to the shop door, locked it and turned the sign around to the closed position. "You'd best come with me."

She was a tiny woman but she held my arm in an iron grip. In her other hand she still carried the knife. I slowly backed into the workroom and collapsed onto an old chair by the side of the door. She stood over me, the sharp blade of the knife resting against the side of my neck. I had always thought of her as small and frail, but for the first time I noticed the whipcord muscles in her arms. My purse was snatched from my hand and she quickly rooted through it until she found my cell phone which went into the pocket of her white overall.

"Where is Doris? What have you done with her?" I tried to stop my voice from shaking.

"It was her own fault, she kept hammering on the door. I told her we weren't open yet but she pushed her way in and she saw him."

"Who?"

"Bert, my husband," she added by way of explanation. "He knew, you see."

"Knew what?"

"That I was the one who killed him."

"Him?"

She seemed exasperated. "You know, the man in the barn."

"You killed him and…"

"That too!" She noted my shocked face and went on calmly, "It was what he deserved. Then I tried to kill the youth minister at church but some women came in to do the altar flowers and I couldn't finish it like I wanted to. So he's not dead yet. After the first one, Bert found out what I'd done. He said I couldn't do no more, but I had to do the other one. David wanted me to, and Bert was going to tell on me."

She sounded like a plaintive child. I took a deep breath and tried to speak in a calm and soothing voice. "Where is Bert now?"

She used the knife to point towards the large walk-in freezer. "In there."

"Is he…?"

"Probably. If he isn't by now, he should be soon."

This was surreal. Ada was discussing the most horrendous things as serenely as if we were chatting over a cup of tea.

I nodded towards Doris' purse. "Where's Mrs.Weppler?"

"She's in there, too."

My heart almost stopped beating. "Did you…?"

"No. I'm just going to leave her in there."

"Ada," I said softly, "she hasn't done anything wrong."

She looked puzzled. "She knows what I did to Bert."

"But she's always been a friend to you."

"What else can I do?"

I kept my voice soft and tried to reason with her. "Then, there's me. My friends know I'm here. If I'm not home soon with Doris, they'll call the police. There's no way they won't search the whole shop."

Ada rubbed her face with her free hand. "I don't know…I don't know…" The hand continued its circular motion. I watched the thought process move across her face. She pointed at me with the knife. "Stand up. I'll put you in there too."

She gestured for me to walk ahead. I could feel the tip of the knife pressing against my ribs. I frantically looked around, searching for something I could use as a weapon. Doris' purse was still on the floor by the side of the freezer. I came near to it and pretended to trip. As

I went down I slipped my hand inside. It closed upon a small, hard object. I pulled it out and tried to conceal it in my pocket.

Ada bent over me. "Drop it." I felt the point of the knife pierce the side of my neck. I let Doris' taser fall to the floor.

"Now get up."

Slowly, I hauled myself to my feet, holding onto the table as if I were going to fall again. My hand moved towards the frozen leg of lamb lying among the other cuts of meat on the table top. I grabbed the narrow end, swung around, and using it like a club, hit her on the side of the head. She staggered. The knife caught my sweater. I felt the burn on my skin so I clubbed her again. This time she went down and stayed there. I ran for the freezer and flung open the door. The butcher was propped up against the wall and huddled in his arms inside his jacket, with just the tips of her gray curls poking out of the top, was a pale and shivering Doris.

Chapter 40

"I felt sorry for her until she locked me in the freezer with her husband."

Doris had her feet up on my sofa and a blanket wrapped around her, but she still looked pale. The ER doctor had wanted her to stay overnight but she insisted on checking herself out of the hospital. She had finally agreed to delay her party for one day after I convinced her neither of us was up for entertaining yet.

"The food is all ready and I'm not going to let it go to waste. Though where I'll be able to get the hams and seafood I don't know."

"Maybe the butcher will open the shop for you today," I offered.

She shuddered. "No thank you. I'll never be able to eat anything that comes out of that freezer again."

"Do you want to tell me what happened?"

I'd seen little of Doris after she was whisked away to the hospital. The butcher was taken in one ambulance and a white-faced, shivering Doris in another. As soon as he heard, Sam had rushed to the shop even though he was supposed to be confined to desk duty. He saw the blood on my sweater and drove me to the hospital where he'd found a doctor to look at the shallow knife wound on my side, which was barely more than a scratch. Once we found that Doris was going to be fine and had checked herself out of the hospital, he insisted I go home and rest. I didn't need to rest and insisted on staying with Doris to take care of her. There had been an argument. I won and hadn't seen him since.

"The doctors told me Bert saved my life by putting me inside his coat. Otherwise I'd have frozen to death. His body heat kept me alive." She added, "And my body heat helped him."

I couldn't imagine Doris' tiny frame generating enough heat to keep a sparrow alive but I nodded anyway. "Did the doctor say how long it will be before you're fully recovered?"

"I'm already recovered, nothing wrong with me. The butcher—his name's Bertram, by the way—isn't that a nice name, Bertram? He said that after their son was killed in a road accident, Ada had a complete mental breakdown. For weeks she couldn't even go into his room. When she finally did, she found a letter in his bedside table. He wrote about the abuse and said he was going to the first victim's barn to confront him, and then he was going to the church to talk to the youth minister."

"Did he give a reason? I can guess about the man in the barn. But the youth minister—did he...?"

"No. They all went to the same church and the man—Stephen's uncle—the first one who was killed— invited David—that was Bert's son's name, over to ride his horses." She sighed. "It was just like what happened to Stephen. David never told anyone neither. He only went there the one time but as he got older it preyed on his mind more and more and he started drinking. His mother asked the youth minister at church to counsel him but when David told him about the abuse, the minister didn't believe him. He said the man was a church member and a good Christian and David should be ashamed to spread such lies about him. The night of the accident David had been drinking again and took the curve on Acton road too fast. The car went into a tree and he was thrown out and killed."

"Doris, she was such a frail looking little woman—how could she do it? And why try to kill her husband?"

"After the first murder, she told him what the man had done. Bert wasn't going to say anything. I think he felt the man deserved it. But when she attacked the youth minister in the church, he told me he had to stop her. They argued. She waited until he went into the freezer, followed him and stabbed him in the back. The heavy jacket he always wore when he worked in there saved his life. The knife didn't hit anything vital and the cold temperatures slowed the bleeding."

"Why put you in the freezer? Why didn't she let you pick up your order and leave?"

"Because I saw him. I heard groans coming from the back room. She tried to stop me but I went in there anyway. I saw a foot sticking out of the freezer door and went over to see what it was. She pushed me in there and slammed the door shut."

She shuddered. "That's when Bertram told me the freezer was one of the old kind that couldn't be opened from the inside. He made me bundle up in his jacket. He said the body heat would help both of us. He was right but I'm glad you got there when you did. I don't know how much longer we could have held out."

"What did the doctors say about your condition?"

"I'm fine but another hour or two and it would have been a different story."

"And the butcher?"

"His ears were frostbit and he lost some blood but the knife wound wasn't that deep. I don't think her heart was in it. She was the one who slaughtered the hogs on their farm, so she should have known exactly how to kill someone."

She took another sip of the hot toddy I'd made for her. "Kate, you remember that day when we heard them arguing in the back of the shop? Bertram never hit her like we thought. She was the one who hit him."

The doorbell rang. It was my son-in-law, Andrew.

Chapter 41

As I led Andrew up the stairs to my apartment, he said, "You have to tell Ellie to give up this ridiculous notion of going back to school."

I stopped and turned around to face him. He was three steps below me and I could tell that my looking down at him made him uncomfortable.

"Ellie isn't going *back* to school—she never went to college in the first place. Why is the idea of her taking classes so threatening to you?"

He couldn't look me in the eye. Instead he sputtered slightly, "She has children to raise."

"You *both* have children to raise and if you want to do it together, I suggest you don't fight her on this."

That shut him up and he followed me into the apartment in silence. Doris and her blanket had disappeared from the couch. Nevertheless, I took Andrew down the hallway into the kitchen and sat opposite him at the table.

"Andrew, what are you afraid of?"

He tried to argue. "I'm not afraid. She says she wants to train for a job but I don't understand why. My father worked to support the family and my mother stayed home and took care of the house. They've been happily married for almost thirty-five years."

"They stay together, Andrew, because your father needs the cloak of respectability that a long term marriage provides. Your mother stays because she's financially dependent on your father and would be too scared to be on her own."

He stood up, red-faced and angry. "I don't know what you are talking about."

"I'm talking about your father's cheating with other women every chance he gets. Your mother knows about the affairs but prefers to live in denial."

In spite of the limited space, Andrew started to pace up and down the kitchen. "I admit my father has gotten a little out of line in the past..."

I was tired of his quibbling. "Having affairs inside a marriage is not getting 'a little out of line.' If you want your relationship with Ellie to survive, I suggest you do everything you can to support her. She is going to college and if you fight her on this it will be the end of your marriage. You're supposed to be her husband, an equal partner, not some autocratic, Victorian father figure."

He stopped in mid-stride, opened his mouth to answer me, thought better of it, stomped back down the hall and out the front door.

Doris poked her head around the dining room door where she had been listening to the entire conversation. "Well, you told him, Kate."

Chapter 42

Thanks to the Senior Center, Doris finally had her party. They turned up early Sunday morning, bearing hams, and covered dishes, and by noon everything was ready. We opened up all three apartments; there was food everywhere and I finally got some room in my refrigerator. Doris was a little upset that she couldn't make her seafood risottos but as I told her, there was plenty for everyone.

I never did get an exact count but people were all over the house, in Enid and Rose's apartment and throughout Doris' and mine. The food disappeared fast and as soon as a dish ran low it was replenished by Doris' intrepid seniors. Ellie came, trailed by a sheepish-looking Andrew who did his best to avoid me.

As I hugged her, she said, "I told him I'm expected to visit his family, so he's going to visit mine."

Andrew walked over to the window and stayed there. Ellie mingled and talked. For the rest of the time they were there it stayed that way.

A few people asked after Pamela Moore but all they got from Doris was the tight-lipped response. "She wasn't invited." And with that they had to be content.

I was happy to see Mira and Ellie in an animated conversation. I overheard Ellie ask, "What exactly do you do in the DA's office?" When I enquired about Kevin, I got a shoulder shrug and a one word answer, "Work."

Sylvia actually brought a date.

"Didn't I see him at one of Rose's art exhibits?"

She giggled. "Yes, that night I let him think he'd been stood up. Well," she added defensively, "he'd just been divorced and I figured he'd be too needy but I ran into him at Enid's show and we got to talking... Anyway, he's a really nice guy."

The nice guy was deep in conversation with another of our library volunteers and with a hurried, "Excuse me," Sylvia rushed to his side.

Sebastian and Stephen were practically joined at the hip. Stephen looked happier than I'd ever seen him. Doris was right, as she usually was. There'd be an announcement any day now.

The person I really wanted didn't come. I checked every time I heard the front door open but Sam was nowhere to be found. I was clearing away the food dishes on one of the buffet tables when I felt a pair of arms encircle my waist. The party was virtually over. Frank was rounding up the stragglers and Doris, Rose, Enid and I were starting on the clean up.

I turned to Sam. "Are you hungry?"

He laughed. "Now you sound like Doris."

"Well, if I know you, you've been at the precinct all day and haven't eaten a thing."

He shrugged his shoulders. "I wouldn't say no to some of that food you're clearing away."

I led him into the kitchen and fixed a hearty plate of leftovers for him. He sat down at the table and started to inhale the food.

"What happened to Ada Fletcher? Has she been arrested?"

Sam started to answer but one of Doris' seniors came into the kitchen with a handful of dirty dishes. He stopped talking immediately. She put the plates on the counter and hurried away only to be replaced by another woman bearing a heavy load.

I sighed. There was no way we could have a private conversation and he looked exhausted. "Sam, it will be another couple of hours before we're through here. Why don't you take a nap in the bedroom and I'll wake you when we're done?"

He stuffed a healthy portion of pineapple upside down cake in his mouth. "Good idea."

He almost stumbled out of the doorway and I heard the bedroom door close. When I went in a couple of hours later, he was in a deep sleep so I didn't wake him. And when I woke up the next morning he'd already left.

Chapter 43

Sam called me. "Kate, any chance you could meet me for lunch?"

We arranged to meet at the deli on the square. As I parked the car, I saw Sam going in the front door. A couple of minutes later, Barbara Armstrong came out of the same door and almost bumped into me in her haste. She didn't acknowledge me in any way, just hurried off down the street.

San was sitting at a corner table. He rose when I came in and gave me a brief hug. He started to say something but was interrupted by the waitress. After ordering, he reached across the table and took one of my hands.

"Kate, I need to talk to you."

The tips of his ears were red, a sure sign he was embarrassed. "Mira says I'm too controlling and if I am, I apologize. I don't mean to be it's just that…"

The waitress interrupted again by delivering our food and after being assured we had everything we needed she finally left us alone.

"Sam, it…"

He stopped me. "Please just let me say it. We argue because Mira says I'm not good at communication. I worry about you Kate, a lot. It's not that I think you need someone to take care of you, it's that I see a lot of bad things that you don't know about…" He took a deep breath and choked out, "Sometimes, I'm scared of losing you."

I started to say something but he interrupted me again, "All that business about Dusty was not because I didn't believe you. First you were going to spend a whole summer away from me and then you were going to be with an old boyfriend. I was jealous. It was something new for me and I didn't know how to handle it. I want our relationship to work. I promise you I'll do better."

I was touched. "I want that too, Sam. And I'll try to be more understanding."

He squeezed my hand then changed topics, "I know you and Doris both want to know how the case is progressing."

I nodded. The first thing Doris asked when I told her Sam and I were meeting for lunch was to be sure and find out what was happening with Bertram, as she called him, and his wife.

"Ada Fletcher is now in a psychiatric facility until she's judged competent enough to stand trial. Her husband has not been charged with anything so far."

"So far?"

"The AG might argue that by not reporting the first murder he bears responsibility for the attack on the youth counselor. The poor man may have been guilty of poor judgment but that's hardly a killing offense."

"Except, that by not believing the youth he was counseling, he may have inadvertently caused his death."

"Because?"

"Because, if someone *had* believed him, David Fletcher might not have gotten drunk that day and crashed his car."

Sam shook his head. "Are we arguing again?"

I laughed. "I'd call it more of a rational discussion."

"I have one more piece of news for you then I have to get back to work."

Sam looked rather pleased with himself. "We know who slashed your tires."

'Which one was it, Bitch Barbara or Pamela Moore?"

"Neither."

"Neither?"

"You know a Cynthia Schwartz?"

"Yes, she was another team leader on the dig."

Sam slowly nodded his head, a big grin on his face.

"You mean she was the one who slashed my tires? How did you find out?"

"It wasn't any brilliant deduction on my part. Two other people in Bloomington had their tires slashed recently—Dawna Sinclair and Leslie Broughton."

"Dawna, Leslie and I were on the same team on the dig."

"That's not all you had in common, right?"

Then it made sense. "We all went out with Adrian, and Cynthia was madly jealous of anyone he showed an interest in."

Sam took a hearty bite of his pastrami sandwich and swallowed it before I got the rest of the story.

"She evidently followed Adrian to Shelbyville the weekend your tires were slashed for the first time. When she saw you and him having dinner together, where he was flirting outrageously with you," Sam tried not to frown but failed, "she found your car in the parking lot and slashed your tires. The day she left Bloomington, she was stupid enough to do the same thing to the two students' cars. But this time she was caught on the school's security cameras. By then she was on her way home to Michigan. She stopped in Shelbyville, found your car in Luigi's parking lot and decided to vandalize it again."

Sam's phone pinged. He listened for a moment, gave a brief, "Be right there," and turned to me.

Before he could say anything, I stood, "I've got it, Sam, you have to leave."

He caught my arm to stop me. "Kate, I know I moved back into my place but…"

I kissed his cheek. "I'll leave the light on for you."

THE END

ABOUT THE AUTHOR

Trisha Durrant was raised in post-war Britain. After seeing an ad in the *London Times*, which said, 'Come to the sun-drenched desert of Arizona,' she immediately decided to emigrate. In her defense, it was raining at the time and she was an out of work actor who was tired of waiting on tables. Now, four children, eight grandchildren and too many cats to enumerate, later, she lives in beautiful Asheville, North Carolina, with her remaining cat, Monty, nicknamed 'The Monster.' *Body in the Barn* is the second book in her Kate and Doris Mystery series.

www.ingramcontent.com/pod-product-compliance
Lightning Source LLC
Chambersburg PA
CBHW020336260626
47156CB00004B/1562